MARRIAGE A LA MODE

By the standards of aristocratic London, the marriage between the Earl of Allandale and Catherine Renwick seemed the most perfect of pairings. After all, both of them each had the perfect partner.

The Earl had ravishing, superbly sensual Lady Caroline Amberly not only as his mistress but she was passionately in love with him.

Catherine had her childhood sweetheart, Ian Maxwell, still totally enamored of her and willing to devote himself to her happiness.

What more could a married couple want?

The answer came as a shock—not only to Regency gossips, but to a husband and a wife fighting against their own uninvited desires. . . .

THE COUNTERFEIT MARRIAGE

THE COUNTERFEIT MARRIAGE

JOAN WOLF

A SIGNET BOOK

SIGNET
Published by the Penguin Group
Penguin Books USA Inc., 375 Hudson Street,
New York, New York 10014, U.S.A.
Penguin Books Ltd, 27 Wrights Lane,
London W8 5TZ, England
Penguin Books Australia Ltd, Ringwood,
Victoria, Australia
Penguin Books Canada Ltd, 10 Alcorn Avenue,
Toronto, Ontario, Canada M4V 3B2
Penguin Books (N.Z.) Ltd, 182–190 Wairau Road,
Auckland 10, New Zealand

Penguin Books Ltd, Registered Offices:
Harmondsworth, Middlesex, England

Published by Signet, an imprint of New American Library,
a division of Penguin Books USA Inc.

First Printing, February, 1980
12 11 10 9 8 7 6 5 4

 REGISTERED TRADEMARK—MARCA REGISTRADA

Printed in the United States of America

I

By our first strange and fatal interview,
By all desires which thereof did ensue,
By our long starving hopes, by that remorse
Which my words' masculine persuasive force
Begot in thee . . .

—JOHN DONNE

"Dammit, Matt, no!" The Earl of Allandale raised his eyes from the glass of wine in front of him and directed a light gray stare at his friend. "If you hadn't let yourself be distracted by that bloody girl, we wouldn't be stuck here in the first place. Dumping us in a ditch like two yokels!"

"Your self-esteem was the only thing hurt, my boy. They'll have that wheel fixed by tomorrow, and we can be on our way." Captain Matthew Armstrong regarded his friend shrewdly. "Though from what I can see, Jamie, you've no great wish to be heading back to London."

Allandale's hand was arrested in the act of raising his glass. Slowly he returned it to the table. "What do you mean, Matt?" he said carefully.

"I mean, lad, that the whole time we were in Scotland you were in fine fettle. But as soon as we turned our back on the heather and the fish, you turned into an oyster." Captain Armstrong looked indigant. "You were in a foul mood, my boy, long before I drove you into that ditch. Why do you think I felt the need for some additional conversation? Unfortunately, it wasn't me she was interested in. They never are," he added gloomily, "when I'm with you, Jamie."

Silence fell as the Earl continued to drink methodically, only pausing to signal for a new bottle. Matt watched him worriedly. It was easy to see what women found to attract them in James Pembrook, sixth Earl of Allandale. His Indian-black hair fell in disorder over his forehead and almost touched the long black lashes that concealed his eyes. Those eyes, light gray and startling in his tanned face, had worn a look the last few days that made Matt extremely uneasy.

They were an odd pair, the slender aristocrat who moved with the grace of a hunting cat, and the tall, burly Scotsman. Matt had met Allandale during the Talavera campaign into Spain in 1809. When the dirty, ragged Spaniard whom Matt had rescued from ambush had turned out to be the Englishman responsible for the awesome task of coordinating Spanish guerrilla activity, Matt had become his devoted follower. Released from official duty to act as aide to young Allandale, Matt had become an expert in passing undiscovered over Spanish terrain, carrying messages between Wellington in Portugal and his brilliant young tactician in Spain.

Matt worshipped Allandale. But he didn't understand him. And he feared the mood of black despair that had been slowly creeping up on Allandale ever since they had turned their backs on Scotland.

"I was damn glad to have you leave the gay life in London and pay me a visit on my native soil, Jamie. But, aside from your understandable desire for my brilliant company, what made you want to come?"

Allandale's mouth twisted into something that was not really a smile. "I was bored, Matt," he said. And poured himself another glass of wine.

"Do you know what I think, Jamie? I think you miss the war."

Allandale rested his forehead on his hands and stared down at the table. His voice, when it came, was muffled. "God, Matt, I hope not." There was a moment's silence, then he continued unwillingly. "In a way, though, the war did give me something I had really never had before."

Matt's voice was gentle. "And what was that, lad?"

The gray eyes opposite him were brilliant. "A reason for living, Matt," the sixth Earl of Allandale, handsome, rich, and well-born, said with blunt, matter-of-fact sincerity.

Matt, twenty years Allandale's senior and counting himself lucky to be still among the roster of the living, shook his head with incomprehension.

"I beg your pardon, my lord." The innkeeper approached their table. "The wheel of your phaeton will be fixed by tomorrow morning, my lord. You may leave right after breakfast."

"Well, now," Matt blustered, "that's good news, Jamie. We can be off early, and I'll be in York to take care of my business by tomorrow. Why don't you go meet that lass by the Roman Wall, like she said, and I'll . . ."

He stopped as Allandale's voice cut him off. "Landlord! Another bottle, if you please."

"Quit the drinking, Jamie." Matt's voice was urgent. He had never seen Allandale drink like this before, and the Earl's single-minded intensity made him nervous. "Come on, Jamie, she was a very taking little thing." He reached out and tried to remove the glass from his friend's hand. Quick fingers, closing on his wrist, numbed his arm. The look on Allandale's face reminded Matt vividly of his years in Spain; the last few weeks of easy comradeship in Scotland were wiped out. The even voice, edged with anger, was the one that Matt had always obeyed. "Stop playing the bloody nursemaid, Matt. If I want to drink, I'll drink." Allandale's voice was bleak and reserved. Slowly, Matt accepted the glass he was holding out.

"All right, lad." Matt's voice was reluctant. "Let's drink."

Catherine Renwick tied her light brown hair back

with a ribbon and pulled an old, faded dress over her
head. The dress had been outgrown years ago, but
Catherine cherished the freedom its short, skimpy skirt
gave her long legs. Tiptoeing carefully, she left her
room and crept down the staircase to the front door.
Two minutes later she was in the stables, bridling a
beautiful chestnut gelding. Dispensing with a saddle,
she vaulted as easily as a boy onto the horse's back,
guiding him with her knees as they left the stable yard.

It was a beautiful morning. The rolling hills and
moors of Northumberland stretched away, green except
for the wildflowers' sprinkling of blue and yellow and
pink. The sky blazed a brilliant blue, with a few high,
white clouds slowly drifting along. The girl moved forward on her horse as he approached a small stream
and he cleared it with an easy motion. Catherine
dropped her hands, and the chestnut lengthened his
stride into a full gallop, the girl so much a part of his
flight that she was almost hidden in the flying mane.
Eventually the headlong gallop slowed as the horse, his
initial burst of energy burned up, moved from run to
canter to slow trot. Catherine patted his sweating neck,
and, with a swift motion, lay back on the glossy hide,
her face turned up to the early morning sun.

She drew in a deep, blissful breath, savoring the
smell of earth and grass, and closed her eyes. For the
past six days Catherine had been confined to the house
by a sore throat. At first she had felt really ill, feverish,
and unable to swallow without severe pain. But by
Tuesday morning she was better, and by yesterday she
was beginning to feel like a trapped animal. Except for
the strange fact that she had lost her voice, she was
perfectly fine, she thought in silent justification of her
unauthorized morning outing. Experimentally, she tried
to speak and the result was the same distressing hoarse
croak. The doctor had assured them that it was a
purely temporary loss, but Catherine found her en-
forced silence more difficult to bear than the pain of
the sore throat had been.

Her father would be furious with her. But to Catherine, soaking up the sun and inhaling the early morning scents, her morning's freedom was worth a scolding. Slowly horse and girl wended their way inevitably toward the Roman Wall just outside the small town of Haltwhistle.

Matthew Armstrong steadied himself with his hand on the wall built by Hadrian so many centuries ago. His eyes were not quite focused, and his breath was heavy with wine. Reduced by alchohol to elementary logic, his brain was preoccupied with just one thing. Must find that lass for Jamie. Even when sober, Matt tended to see life's problems simply and his solution was usually the same—a woman. It was obvious that Allandale was in a vile mood. Matt was going to help him out. Quite simple, really—except, thought Matt, angrily scanning the horizon, there was no girl in sight.

At this point in his foggy meditations, a chestnut horse appeared on the crest of the hill. As Matt peered blearily, he saw the figure of a girl sit up on the horse's back and look his way. The glossy brown gelding came closer and Matt was able to take in the long slender legs, bared to the knees, the old dress and long fall of brown hair that was Catherine. Stepping out from the shadow of the wall, he signaled to her unevenly.

Catherine was startled by the sudden appearance of the man. From his urgent, uncertain motions, it appeared he was in trouble. Perhaps hurt. She slid off her horse easily, dropped the reins over his head, and moved swiftly toward the man in distress. As she reached him, a look of concern on her face, Matt reached out and grabbed her arm.

"Well met, lassie. I knew I could depend on you."

Matt's grip grew tighter as Catherine tried to pull away. "Don't worry, lass. I'm going to take you to him. Jamie had a bit of a . . . well, he was delayed, and I've come to fetch you for him. Everything's all right and tight, eh?"

His eyes, as he looked at Catherine, were strangely unfocused. She struggled with him in mixed alarm and anger. Who was this clod who dared to lay a hand on her? She opened her mouth to tell him exactly what she thought of him—and nothing came out. Only a hoarse croak.

Matt was too preoccupied to notice. When he started to lift her onto his horse, Catherine began to fight in earnest. Surprised by her reaction, Matt pinioned her with two powerful hands and somehow got the two of them on his horse.

"We're going to him. Dammit, stop scratching me. Bloody little wildcat."

With all her strength, Catherine fought to break the hold that crushed her to the chest of the man behind her. Then, viciously, she used her heels on the horse. The animal bolted, only to be brought up short by an iron hand on the bridle. Swiftly, Catherine's arm was drawn up behind her back. Excruciating pain shot through her arm and shoulder.

"Listen to me, girl. If you don't want your arm broken for you, you'll calm down. Do you hear what I say?"

Through the stabbing pain, Catherine's bent head nodded. Her arm was lowered just a little.

"Good. I'm not kidnapping you. I'm just taking you to meet the gentleman you made an appointment with earlier this evening. So be a good girl, and stop making me hurt you."

Catherine's mind was in a whirl. What was he talking about? What gentleman? Oh God, she thought frantically, he had mistaken her for someone else. Why couldn't she talk! With an effort that was almost physical, she forced herself to think calmly. Once this "gentleman" saw her, he would know there had been a mistake. He would send for Papa, and there would be an end of it.

"Are you going to stop fighting now?" Matt's voice, slurred and borne on a distinctly winey breath, was at her ear. Taking a deep breath, Catherine nodded.

"Good girl." The cruel grip was slackened, and Matt

turned his attention to their direction. "We're almost there, anyway."

A few moments later, Matt and Catherine rode into the Border Maid courtyard. Desperately, Catherine searched for a sign of life. They knew her here. If only someone would come! But it was too early. Matt left the horse standing in the courtyard and led her through the empty public rooms of the inn. Up the stairs they went, Catherine vainly trying to produce some sound through her constricted throat.

Matt stopped in front of a door and knocked. There was no answer. Matt knocked again. "Jamie, lad. I've got something for you."

There was no sound inside the room. but suddenly the door was thrown open. Inimical gray eyes stared at them. "Matt," a carefully controlled voice said, "I warned you . . ."

"I know you did, lad. But sometimes, you know, I don't listen. Here's a little lady who's been pining for your company." Catherine found herself pushed into the room, and the door closed behind Matt, leaving her with this somehow terrifying stranger.

He was looking at her, an odd brilliance in his eyes. "I wasn't thinking along these lines, my dear. But then, I also never like to disappoint a lady." He came closer to her. "Particularly a lady as beautiful as you." His eyes raked her mercilessly. "Well, go ahead, take off your clothes."

Catherine's eyes dilated in horror. What was he talking about? This couldn't be happening, she thought in panic, it was all some horrible mistake. Whirling around. she reached for the door handle.

"I don't think so, my lovely. I think you had better stay here with me." Allandale's eyes, fever-bright from drink, looked into Catherine's, gray also, but alive and terrified.

He gave a twisted smile. "Maybe Matt was right. after all. He often is, damn him. Don't be shy, darling. You'll be well paid for your trouble."

Catherine felt herself lifted in his arms and deposited

on the bed. Stunned, almost numb from fear and confusion, she dimly perceived that he was taking off his clothes.

No no no no no! her mind kept screaming frantically. But she couldn't say anything! With a quick movement, she rolled over in an attempt to get off the bed and make it to the door. A relentless hand grabbed her arm and dragged her back.

"Too late to change your mind now. You shouldn't have come with Matt if you didn't want to play." A man's heavy weight crushed her and a mouth, smelling of wine, came down over hers. She opened her mouth to breathe, and a rough tongue was pushed in instead. She was suffocating! When his mouth left hers for a moment, she could make no sound but the same harsh croak.

He didn't seem to notice. His hands, impatient of the constrictions of her garments, began to rip and tear. Oh God! Oh God! Catherine redoubled her efforts to throw him off, to scratch, to maim—anything to get this thing off of her.

As she sought in silent desperation, helpless against the strength that held her, he ripped through the thin chemise that was her only undergarment for the morning's ride, and his mouth found her smooth skin. Catherine got her hands deep in his hair and pulled frantically. He laughed, seemingly insensible of the hurt she was inflicting. He pinioned down her twisting body with his superior weight and with strong, inexorable hands, forced her legs open. A moment later a terrible burning pain went through her. Her body convulsed, in an effort to get away from the pain he was causing her, but she was powerless to move. Her throat worked vainly in an effort to scream. She couldn't breathe. Her breath wheezed in her constricted throat as she struggled for air. Sheer, mindless terror took possession of Catherine. She hurt herself badly in her mad efforts to throw him off, but she was helpless. Allandale appeared to be oblivious to her distress. Things began to go black in front of her eyes and she lost consciousness. A few moments later, the Earl, thinking her asleep, dragged a blanket from the bed, wrapped himself in it, and lay down to sleep in front of the fireplace.

Catherine lay unconscious for about fifteen minutes. She woke to find the horror she had hoped she dreamed was in fact a frightening reality. The sheets were stained with blood. Blood and something else was running down her legs. Her clothes were in tatters. And over on the floor, in front of the fireplace, slumbered the man who had done this to her.

Wrapping herself in the other blanket, Catherine crept silently to the door and let herself out. Standing in the hall, she began to shake uncontrollably, not knowing what to do next. It was in this state that she was found by Mrs. Morely, the landlord's wife.

"Miss Renwick! What happened?"

Catherine just shook her head and continued to tremble violently.

"Who did this to you?" The horrified landlady looked at the closed door behind the girl. But at the anguished expression on Catherine's face, she simply gathered the distraught girl into her arms. "There, there, my dear. It will be all right. You just come with me. That's right now. . . ." Cajoling softly, Mrs. Morely gently moved Catherine down the corridor toward the stairs. Moving slowly because Catherine's shaking knees threatened to give way, Mrs. Morely finally got her to her private sitting room. She put Catherine into a chair, and slipped out into the hallway.

"John," she spoke in a low tone to her husband, already at work in the tap room. "Ride out to Renwick Hall for Sir Francis. His daughter's in our sitting room, and unless I'm much mistaken, something dreadful has happened to her."

He opened his mouth to speak, but she shook her head. "Never mind, now. Just get him." He looked at her face, nodded, and turned toward the stables. Mrs.

Morely went back to Catherine and, speaking quietly, began to wash her still trembling body.

When the landlord arrived at Renwick Hall, he found it in an uproar. Catherine's horse had come home alone, and her father was about to ride out in search of her. Mr. Morely's arrival halted him.

"Catherine is at the Border Maid?" Sir Francis's normally gentle expression was darkened by something in between anger and fear. "What is she doing there at this hour of the morning? She's not hurt, is she?"

But Mr. Morely had no information to give him, except that he was to come at once. Sir Francis's brows drew together. He was a very handsome man, with a wide, thoughtful brow and dark blond hair streaked with white. He was a scholar who spent his spare time running the various farms that made up his estate. The only thing Sir Francis loved more than his books was his daughter. And, looking at Morely's face, he had a deeply uneasy feeling that something was very wrong with her. "Let us go immediately, Morely," he said tersely, and mounting his horse, led the way down the drive.

Mrs. Morely regarded Catherine in deep concern. She was wrappd in an old cloak of the landlady's and the external signs of what had happened to her had been removed. The shaking had stopped, but Mrs. Morely thought the lifeless, empty look in her eyes was even worse. She looked up in fear at the sudden noise outside the room, but her expression altered as soon as she saw who it was. "Papa!" Her lips formed the word, but no sound came. Sir Francis took one look at the expression on his daughter's face, and went pale himself.

"Cathy, my love," he went forward and she rose and flung herself into his arms. Frightened by her silent weeping, he looked at Mrs. Morely. "What happened? Was she trapped somewhere?"

"In a manner of speaking, Sir Francis," the landlady returned. "I found her in the upstairs hall, outside one of the bedrooms. She had been raped."

"What!" the words ripped from Sir Francis's throat. "Is this true, Cathy?"

The silky brown head, buried in his shoulder, nodded.

"Oh my God!" his voice shook with emotion. "Who would do such a thing?"

"Was it the gentleman in the room you was outside of, Miss Renwick?" Mrs. Morely inquired gently.

A shudder ran through Catherine's slender body, but once again she nodded.

"That bloody bastard," the quiet, scholarly Sir Francis." Mrs. Morely's tone was pragmatic. "I think you body of his only daughter, "I'll kill him."

"Killing him isn't going to solve anything, Sir Francis." Mrs. Morely's tone was pragmatic. "I think you should take Miss Renwick home first, then come back here to talk to this Earl."

"Earl?" Sir Francis's eyes widened in surprise.

"Aye, Sir Francis," Mrs. Morely said meaningfully, "the Earl of Allandale."

At her words. Catherine shrank even closer to her father. Sir Francis rested his cheek for a moment, consolingly, against her hair. "All right my love. Don't worry, Papa is taking you home." He walked her slowly to the door. At the threshold he turned to face the landlady. "I will be back shortly, Mrs. Morely. Don't allow the Earl of Allandale to leave until I return."

She nodded soberly. "That'll be best, Sir Francis. Rapes sometimes have consequences, you know."

The ride home seemed to Catherine almost unreal. The morning was just as beautiful as it had been two hours ago, when she raced her horse across the moors. But the ugliness of what had just occurred put a gap forever between the carefree child of this morning and the shocked, silent girl who sat cradled in her father's arm as his horse moved slowly through the sunshine. Going through her mind with monotonous regularity was a single refrain. *Nothing will ever be the same again.*

II

O thou foul thief, where hast thou stowed my daughter?
—WILLIAM SHAKESPEARE

Sir Francis rode back to the Border Maid, rage and bewilderment warring in his mind. He had left Catherine in the care of their housekeeper, and the memory of his daughter's face was a knife in his breast.

How could this have happened? Why? Why to Catherine, the sweetest, most gentle . . . Sir Francis's hands shook as he struggled to get hold of himself. He must be in control when he interviewed the Earl of Allandale. He must do what was best for Catherine. Mrs. Morely's words, "Rapes sometimes have consequences," were very much on his mind.

Allandale. Sir Francis knew the name well. He had followed carefully the campaign in the Peninsula, and his friend John Mar in the war department had many times sung the praises of the young Earl of Allandale. "A genius for guerrilla warfare," had been Mar's words. "One of the main reasons for Wellington's success." And this was the man responsible for the violation of Sir Francis's daughter.

His horse moved steadily across the Northumberland moors. A bright breeze sent the small white clouds scudding across the sky. The tall fair-haired man rode with the true horseman's slouch, his scholarly brow in contrast to his ease in the saddle. By the time he reached the market town of Haltwhistle, his mind had been made up. The Earl of Allandale would have to marry his daughter.

Allandale and Matt were having a belated breakfast when Sir Francis Renwick entered the coffee room. He had himself under rigid control as he surveyed the two men before him. "Which of you, may I ask, is Lord Allandale?"

"I am, sir." Allandale put down his tankard and raised an inquiring eyebrow. "How may I serve you?"

"It is not, my lord, how you may serve me. It is how you served my daughter that I wish to speak to you about."

"Your daughter?" Allandale's tone was genuinely puzzled. "I'm afraid I don't know what you are talking about."

Sir Francis advanced a few steps farther into the room and studied the face before him. There were shadows of sleeplessness under the remarkable gray eyes, and a pulse throbbing in Allandale's forehead gave testimony to the fact that he was suffering from a severe headache. But Sir Francis suddenly found it difficult to believe that this finely-made young man, with his brilliant war record, could have harmed Catherine. His eyes switched to Matthew Armstrong. That broad, snub-nosed face looked much more capable of such a deed.

Taking a deep breath, Sir Francis spoke bluntly. "I am Sir Francis Renwick of Renwick Hall. I am here to discover who is responsible for the rape of my daughter."

"What!" The word ripped across the room. Allandale rose from his chair, almost knocking it over. "What the devil are you talking about?"

Sir Francis held his gaze. "This morning my young daughter was discovered outside your door, my lord. According to Mrs. Morely, the landlady of this inn, she was shaking and in a state of shock. Her clothing had been ripped from her body." His voice trembled, but he controlled it and continued. "It was quite clear, my lord, that she had been brutally violated."

Allandale's pale gray eyes were narrowed. He spoke softly, but there was something in his voice that set Sir Francis's teeth on edge. "I don't know who you are, sir, or what your game is, but I am no pigeon ripe for plucking. I do not find it necessary to get by force what is easy enough to come by willingly. I think you had better leave."

Sir Francis forced down the anger that threatened to explode inside him. He trained all his judgmental faculties on Allandale, and decided that he was telling the truth. His eyes turned to Matthew Armstrong.

"Don't look at me," Matt protested in alarm. "The only girl I saw all night was that servant lass. Rape isn't my game, either."

Sir Francis recognized the accent that colored Matt's words. "I see, sir, you are from north of the border. From Liddesdale by any chance?"

Matt looked surprised. "Aye. From Newcastleton."

Sir Francis regarded him steadily. "Then you know my daughter's grandfather, Lord Carberry."

"Lord Carberry! Jesus, that old tartar. All of Liddesdale knows him, I imagine." Matt's brow furrowed. A different note crept into his voice. "Your daughter's grandda you say?"

"Yes."

Matt turned to Allandale. "We'd better help Sir Francis clear this matter up, Jamie. Christ, if old Carberry finds out his granddaughter's been raped!" Matt shuddered at the prospect.

Allandale's voice was impatient. "I am very sorry for you, Sir Francis, but I fail to see how we can help you."

Sir Francis said slowly, "There was no girl with either of you last night?"

"Just that servant lass," said Matt. "I fetched her for Jamie. But she was willing, never fear."

"Where did you fetch her from? At what time?"

"From by the Roman Wall, early this morning. She

told Jamie she'd meet him there . . ." Matt's voice trailed off as he saw the look on Sir Francis's face.

"My daughter's horse came home by himself this morning. He came from the direction of the wall."

Impatiently, Allandale shook his head. "I am sorry for you, sir," he repeated. "But any girl I bed is willing. Your daughter, if it *was* your daughter, was not forced against her will. Now that she has been caught out, she may wish you to believe so . . ."

"Lord Allandale," Sir Francis's voice leaped across the few feet that separated them. "My daughter is in a state of shock from the ordeal she was put through. I would have the story from her lips, but she has temporarily lost her voice due to illness. Doubtless," his voice shook with passion, "doubtless that was why she did not cry out." His eyes took in the shadows under Allandale's eyes, the pulse beating in his temple. "Just how sober were you last night, my lord?"

Allandale's black brows drew together. For a moment he stood, his eyes fixed on Sir Francis's face. Then, "I will be back in a moment," and he turned and left the room. When he returned five minutes later, his face was very pale and the pulse in his temple was throbbing even more strongly. He held in his hand a small locket. "Does this belong to your daughter?"

Sir Francis looked grim. "Yes."

Allandale's expressionless gray eyes met the pain-filled ones of the older man. "I fear you are right, Sir Francis."

"What!" Matt was outraged.

Allandale looked at him briefly, "From the looks of the room there appears to have been a struggle." He paused momentarily, then said slowly, "There was blood on the sheets."

"Oh, my God," Sir Francis sat down abruptly and buried his face in his hands.

Allandale's expression was unreadable. "You were correct in your assumption that I was not sober last night, sir."

"Jesus," Matt was horrified. "Lord Carberry's granddaughter!"

Allandale's glance silenced him. His voice clipped and precise, James Pembrook, sixth Earl of Allandale, said, "I will marry your daughter, Sir Francis, if you wish."

Sir Francis looked up. "What kind of a man are you, Lord Allandale? Has the war so brutalized you that you can commit a crime such as this, and not even blink?"

"You appear to know something of me, sir."

"I know your name and your reputation. I wish to God I knew nothing more!"

A flicker passed over Allandale's face. "Sir Francis, I was stinking drunk and I injured a member of your family. I am sorry. I am willing to marry your daughter. What else do you want me to say?"

"Nothing." Sir Francis rose slowly from the table. "I will procure a special license, and you and Catherine will be married tomorrow. Then I want you to go away, my lord. I shall be in touch with you in two months' time. If all is well, I shall have the marriage annulled. Should Catherine be expecting a child . . ." Here his voice broke.

"If that should be the case, Sir Francis," Allandale's tone was cool, "you may rest assured that I shall see to it that your daughter's reputation and the legitimacy of the child shall not be questioned."

The older man's troubled blue eyes met the strangely pale ones of the black-haired man. Slowly he nodded. "Be at Renwick Hall tomorrow at ten."

As the door closed behind Sir Francis, Matt turned to Allandale. "Damme Jamie, are you really going to marry the girl?"

"Christ, Matt!" Allandale's tone was savage. "I could kill you. You threw that damned girl into my room. What the hell was the matter with you?"

Matt was gloomy. "The same thing that was wrong with you, laddie. I was blind drunk." Matt ran his fingers through his hair. "What a mess."

"That is the understatement of the year. Allandale headed for the door himself. "I don't even remember what the bloody girl looked like!"

The weather matched Allandale's mood as he drove out to Renwick Hall next morning. The sky was overcast and threatening, rumbles of thunder came from the distance. The moors, with their scattering of farms, looked bleak and cold. The smell of wet moss was in his nostrils.

Renwick Hall was a square house of gray stone. It looked as though it had sat there for centuries, fronting the border with Scotland. It belonged to people who lived comfortably, but not lavishly. There were chickens in the yard and a beautiful chestnut horse in the paddock in front of the stables.

Sir Francis met Allandale at the front door and took him into the front parlor. The room was cheerful and comfortable. The furniture looked a trifle worn, but the tables held bowls of flowers and books were tucked into every nook and cranny. In front of the wide front window stood a beautiful piano. Allandale mentally compared this room with the elegant, expensive perfection of the drawing room at his own magnificent estate and decided he preferred this one.

He turned to his host. "I take it the bride is willing?"

Sir Francis's mouth was grim. "She has been prevailed upon to accept the purely temporary shelter of your name, my lord. I have promised her to obtain an annullment in two months. No mention was made of the other—er—possibility." Sir Francis's eyes met Allandale's meaningfully.

"Oh, you may rely on me to keep my mouth shut," Allandale replied.

A motherly-looking woman with a worried look on her face appeared. "The Reverend Mr. Alston is here, Sir Francis," she said.

Sir Francis hurried forward, and escorted the clergyman into the room. He introduced the two men, then said, "If you will excuse me, gentlemen, I will get me daughter." Five minutes later he returned, holding the hand of a young girl.

She was pale, with shadows under her smoky gray eyes. Still, nothing could dim Catherine Renwick's beauty. Allandale's eyes opened fully at the sight of her. Her light brown hair, shot through with threads of gold, was simply brushed back from her face and hung down her back like heavy silk. Her face had the classical perfection sometimes seen in Greek sculpture but rarely in life. Her long brown lashes, tipped with gold by the sun, framed eyes as gray and stormy as the day. She didn't look at Allandale at all, but turned to face Mr. Alston.

"Christ!" thought Allandale hilariously. "To think I raped that and was too drunk to even appreciate it."

"My lord?" The ceremony was beginning.

Fifteen minutes later, Allandale was in his carriage once again. He had furnished Catherine's father with his address in London and Sir Francis had engaged to write to him as soon as they knew how things stood with Catherine. By noon, the Earl of Allandale was on his way home to London.

III

It was no dreams I lay broad waking.
But all is turned, thorough my gentleness,
Into a strange fashion of forsaking. . . .

—SIR THOMAS WYATT

Catherine was suffocating, unable to breathe. The walls of the small, dark prison were closing around her. Desperately, she fought for air as they closed in—in—in. "No!" she screamed, and woke shaking, sweating with fear. She lay in bed, fighting to control the sobs that shook her slender body. After a few moments, she rose and opened her curtain to let the moonshine into the room.

This was the sixth time in two months she had had that dream. Catherine had thought she had outgrown her private nightmare, but of late it had come back, more terrifying than ever. It was always the same. She was walking along a narrow, dimly lit corridor. She was afraid. Someone was behind her, but every time she turned to look her eyes saw only emptiness. Suddenly, as she paused, listening for footsteps, all the lights in the corridor went out. Very slowly, the walls started to close in on her. The ceiling lowered, too, as the walls moved. Petrified, she tried to hold them back, but her strength was useless. As the space closed in, she felt her air supply giving out. It was as though someone had placed a pillow over her face, and she struggled to draw air into her lungs. Finally, when she thought she was going to black out, she woke up.

The nightmare had started when Catherine was nine years old. She had crawled into a cave on her grandfather's estate in Scotland and a rock slide had trapped her. It had taken five hours to clear away the rocks and get to her, and ever since then Catherine could not tolerate small, dark places. She had not had the nightmare for over a year, and thought she was free of it, until that horrible day two months ago.

She stood at the window, breathing slowly and deeply, trying to think of nothing but the big bright moon high in the heavens. But other things, fears she had tried to repress, came crowding to the forefront of her mind. The nightmare always brought it back, the terror and pain of her one and only encounter with James Pembrook, sixth Earl of Allandale.

Her father had explained to her. It was partly her fault—out riding with no companion, dressed like a peasant, no voice to cry out with. But what kind of man, Catherine wondered, would do such a thing—even to a poor serving girl? She would not believe that he didn't realize she was fighting him.

The two months since that July morning had passed quietly. Catherine continued her usual activities. She visited the farms, rode, studied with her father, practiced her music. Only she never rode across the border to visit her grandfather. And her grandfather and her cousin Ian stayed away from Renwick Hall. Catherine didn't ask what her father had told them, but she was grateful that they didn't come.

Outwardly, her life was orderly and serene. Inwardly, she was in turmoil. The only sign of that turmoil was the recurring nightmare and the increasing wildness of her gallops across the moors.

She knew very well why her father had insisted she marry Lord Allandale. Catherine was not country bred for nothing. She had agreed because she was confused and fearful and her father had wanted her to. She did not think it was necessary. And, anyway, it was purely temporary.

But for the last few weeks she had been becoming

increasingly fearful. Things were not right with her. Every day she desperately looked for a sign that her fears were unfounded. But nothing came.

She stood at her window, eyes black with terror. For the first time she put into words what she had feared the most. "I am with child."

Later that morning, over breakfast, which Catherine ate sparingly because of the distinctly queasy feeling in her stomach, she said the same thing to her father. "Papa, I think I am going to have a baby." She looked away from the anguished expression in his eyes. "Perhaps I ought to see Dr. Morton."

He nodded painfully. "I'll drive you into town this morning, Cathy."

The look on the doctor's face told Sir Francis all he had to know, as he put his arm around his daughter to escort her to the door. As the old-fashioned chaise moved along slowly, he turned to look at Catherine's profile. Her hair was braided and arranged in a shining crown on her head. Her face was pale under the disgraceful tan she managed to acquire every summer. The simple dress of sprigged muslin only enhanced her look of youth and defenseless innocence. Sir Francis paused to swallow the bitter anger he felt, then spoke gently. "Cathy, Lord Allandale and I discussed the possibility of a child."

Her face never changed. "You did? And what did you decide, Papa?"

"Listen, my darling. He is really not a bad man. I know it's hard for you to understand, but men—good men—sometimes do things they bitterly regret afterwards."

"Do they?" Catherine's tone was expressionless.

"Yes. And Lord Allandale is very sorry for—for what happened. He has promised that he will guard your reputation and acknowledge the child as his."

"How perfectly noble of him."

"Cathy!" Sir Francis was urgent. "I know you are angry—and you've every right to be. But we cannot afford to ignore facts. Do you want to damage your reputation irreparably?"

Catherine looked stonily in front of her. "Damn my reputation."

Sir Francis rubbed his forehead. "Unless this marriage is revealed, your child will be branded a bastard. He could be the next Earl of Allandale, if his mother has the courage to do what is right."

Catherine's head swung around on that. Her gray eyes were stormy. "Papa, do *you* tell me to go live with this man as his wife?"

"You must present at least the appearance of a marriage, Cathy. For your sake, and for the sake of the child you carry. Lord Allandale understands this. We arranged that, if it happened that you should be with child, he would take you to his estate in Somerset. At least until after the birth." Sir Francis leaned toward his daughter in his urgency. "Cathy, your marriage and the child's legal paternity must be established in the eyes of the world, or you and the child will become social outcasts."

Catherine's lovely face remained stony. "Papa, I do not want that man ever to touch me again."

A spasm of pain crossed Sir Francis's face. "I'll speak to him, my darling. I'll make it clear that this marriage is to be one in name only."

"No, Papa," said this new, relentless Catherine. "*I* will speak to him. You may tell him to come, but whether I will agree to this marriage or not will depend on my satisfying myself about his intentions."

Sir Francis nodded slowly. "All right, Cathy. I'll write and tell him to come."

When his lordship of Allandale received Sir Francis Renwick's letter he cursed; then he set about retrieving the situation. No one must ever know how the marriage came about. The truth would be fatal, not only to his reputation, for which he cared not a damn, but to Catherine's as well. James Pembrook felt remorse about very few things in his life, but he regretted what he had done to Catherine. Her family was impeccable. Her father had a considerable reputation as a scholar and was not infrequently mentioned as an authority in the drafting of reform legislation. Her grandfather, Lord Carberry, was in fact an old friend of Allandale's formidable Aunt Louisa. To inflict social ostracism on a girl of Catherine's background was unthinkable.

So Allandale set to work to smooth things over. His own position in the social world was assured. His name and his wealth alone would have guaranteed him acceptance into the highest ranks of Regency society. Added to these assets were his extraordinary good looks and his reputation as a war hero. In fact, Allandale was the biggest thing to hit London since Byron.

He hated it. But its very purposelessness suited his mood. He had fought at Waterloo and stayed on with the army of occupation for some months. In January, he had resigned his commission and come home. He had brought with him Wellington's recommendation that the allied army presently occupying France be considerably reduced.

Allandale had not wanted to be Wellington's messenger, but the Duke had insisted. "You've been in this thing all the way, Allandale. They know you're not soft on France." So he had agreed and concluded his involvement with the war by asking the English cabinet to withdraw its troops from the country he had helped defeat. His dispassionate, impeccably logical presentation had made a deep impression on both the foreign minister, Lord Castlereagh, and his most formidable rival, George Canning. Both made overtures to the young Earl, for they sensed his valuable qualities could be a great addition to a sorely-pressed foreign office. They had both been rejected.

After years of war and treaty negotiations, Allandale plunged into the untried waters of London society; the Regency world of beaux and corinthians, balls and Almacks, Whites and Tattersalls. After years of constant danger, of making decisions that involved life or death, he felt like a displaced person in a world where one's biggest decision was how to tie one's neckcloth.

The war had alienated him from the world inhabited by most young men of his age and social class. The peace had alienated him from the world of international power politics he had entered in the Spanish Peninsula War. For, under the seemingly bored and calm exterior Allandale presented to the world, he seethed with anger at what the victors of the Napoleonic wars had wrought with the Peace Treaty of Vienna.

Allandale's oldest friend, Davy Aberfan, a member of Parliament for Wales, had tried only once to talk to him about it. Allandale's mouth had set in hard, bitter lines. "Don't try to justify it to me, Davy. It was national sentiment that destroyed Napoleon. The people of Spain won that war in the Peninsula. Wellington had to hide in Portugal for years. It was we in Spain who tied down thousands of French troops by unrelenting guerrilla warfare. And let me tell you, Davy," for once the mask that usually hid Allandale's emotions was lifted, and Davy found himself backing away from what he saw revealed in Allandale's gray eyes, "what went on in Spain wasn't pretty. It wasn't the noble pageant between knights in shining armor that was played out by the British and the French." He took a step closer to Davy. "Have you ever seen men sawed up alive and impaled on stakes?" At the look on Davy's face, he smiled bleakly. "No, I thought not. Massacre, rape, torture, all the most bestial passions, that's what I saw in Spain, Davy. Waterloo was a picnic compared to it."

Allandale's eyes, black with emotion, looked directly into Davy's. "And what did Spain get out of it all, my fine member of Parliament? A rotten king who repudiated everything that we fought for the moment he got his crown back. No, my friend. It was the people who overthrew Napoleon, and at Vienna it was the princes who reaped the benefits of his fall. I want nothing to do with any government who was a party to that betrayal." And he had left the room abruptly, leaving Davy, white-faced and shaken, alone in the center of the floor.

The problem was that world affairs were Allandale's natural métier, and, having cut himself off from them, he had nothing left. So he drifted about London, got himself involved in a liaison with Lady Caroline Amberly, and drank.

Sir Francis's letter changed all that and gave Allandale a purpose to work for. In three days' time he had made arrangements to open his town house, something his Aunt Louisa had been after him to do for months. He also sent an urgent missive to his formidable aunt. She was a dragon, but Allandale knew she would do anything for him. And her social consequence was enormous. If Catherine was introduced to London society by the Countess of Lothian, she was made for life. After that, they could go their own ways.

Allandale concluded his unwonted activity by sending a notice to the newspaper announcing his marriage. And, as an afterthought, he dispatched a note to Lady Caroline Amberly. In a well-sprung chaise. suitable for transporting a lady in a delicate situation, he set out for Northumberland and Renwick Hall.

Sir Francis paused for a moment to appreciate the picture his daughter made. She was seated in the orchard under an old and gnarled apple tree. The sun dappled the grass around her and brought out the gold threads in her light brown hair. The girl, her head bent over a book, and the green sunny landscape irresistibly suggested peace, tranquility, and quiet joy. Sir Francis bit his lip and approached his daughter. "Lord Allandale is here, my darling."

Catherine's head came up like that of a startled fawn, and she rose quickly. She drew a deep breath and let it out slowly. "Will you ask him to come out here, Papa?"

"I'll bring him." But Catherine was shaking her head.

"No, Papa. I think it will be best if I see him alone."

Sir Francis looked into the clear, determined eyes of his only child and nodded. "All right, Cathy. I'll send him out."

Catherine sat down again abruptly and forced herself to breathe slowly and deeply. Her chest felt constricted and her stomach began to heave. As she fought a silent battle to get control of herself, Allandale approached her from the house.

In the end it was sheer surprise that conquered Catherine's rising faintness and nausea. He was so different from what she had remembered. She was expecting an enormous, hulking creature. Allandale was of medium height, only a few inches taller than she. He had the look of a man who lived on his nerves, not on his appetites. Gray eyes met gray; the man spoke first. "I appear to have made the most damnable mess of your life. It seems trivial to apologize, but I am most sincerely sorry."

His voice surprised her, too. "Somehow," she said steadily, "that doesn't help much."

"I know. But I mean it, so I thought I'd say it." She continued to look at him, her eyes wide with thought, and he went on. "I've come to take you to Barton Abbey, my estate in Somerset. I've sent a notice of our marriage to the papers and have notified my aunt, who will, I believe, help us to smooth over any initial difficulties our sudden union may cause to arise."

"I see. You and my father have arranged things very neatly, have you not?"

Allandale's expression altered slightly as he took in her words. For the first time it was borne in on him that he was not facing a willing bride. He moved to the bench facing hers and sat down. "What do *you* want, Catherine?" he said evenly.

Her face clouded and she bent her head. "I want the impossible," she said, "to turn back time."

He looked at the girl seated so close to him and felt a brief stab of pity. The bright sunlight drew sparks of gold from her hair and from the long, lowered lashes;

she looked up at him and her eyes were deep and dark with emotion. He caught his breath, then leaned forward and spoke soberly. "Listen to me, Catherine. It is impossible to excuse behavior such as mine, but I want you to know that I never would have taken you like that if I had not thought you were willing. I was very drunk, you know."

Catherine bit her lip. "I know," she said, her voice low. She took a deep breath and spoke with heroic directness. "Lord Allandale, you want me to go with you and to live as your wife. I will do so only if you give me your word of honor that this marriage is to be in name only. I cannot, I will not, live on—" she faltered, "—terms of intimacy with a stranger. And that is what we are to each other, strangers." Her gray eyes were steady on his, judging him for the truth's sake, concerned with the sort of man he really was.

He spoke carefully in return. "You have nothing to fear from me on that score. I will not interfere with you. The marriage is, as you say, in name only."

Very slowly, Catherine's shining brown head nodded agreement. "I believe you," she said, her eyes on the inky black hair, long-lashed eyes, and sensitive mouth of the man who had, through such ugliness, become her husband. She stood up. "Very well, Lord Allandale, I will agree to accompany you to Barton Abbey."

"Excellent," he rose also, his face grave. "I have only one request to make."

Her eyebrows rose a trifle. "What is it?"

"My friends call me James, not Lord Allandale. I should like very much for you to address me by my name and not my title."

For the first time in their brief acquaintance, Catherine smiled. "I should be happy to, James," she said.

As Allandale followed her toward the house, a little punchy from that smile, the thought flashed through his mind that the promise he had just given was going to be damned difficult to keep.

IV

Oh happy man, which dost aspire
To that which seemly thou dost crave.

—SIR EDWARD DYER

Thank you, Mrs. Challoncer, you are most kind."
Catherine smiled at the housekeeper gratefully. "I am
tired, I must confess, and should be glad to rest before
dinner."

"I should think so, my lady. Such a journey you've
had. My lady didn't bring her maid with her?"

A rueful look came into Catherine's eyes. "I'm
afraid, Mrs. Challoncer, that I'm just a simple country
girl used to doing for myself. The splendors of Barton
Abbey will quite overcome me, I'm sure. May I rely on
you to be my guide?"

Mrs. Challoncer, who was well aware that Catherine
was the granddaughter of an Earl, looked skeptical but
pleased. She reminded Catherine of a plump pigeon,
ruffling its feathers. "I'm sure nothing could make me
happier, my lady. Unfortunately, what with my lord
away at war for so long and no Lady Allandale to see
to things, the house staff has been cut back to hardly
anything. Mr. Edgecomb has run the estate for my lord
for so many years now . . . However, I'm sure I can
engage a girl from the village to look after your ladyship until you can get a proper lady's maid."

"That will be fine, Mrs. Challoncer."

"Well, I'll leave you to your rest, my lady." The

housekeeper closed the door gently behind her, leaving Catherine prey to many thoughts.

The journey had been tiring, but not half so bad as she had feared. Thank God, she hadn't been sick. And Allandale had been astonishingly considerate, making sure they stopped frequently for rest and food. At each of the inns where they had stayed, she had had her own room to which she had retired after dinner, only seeing him again at breakfast the next day.

And now she was faced with Barton Abbey, her new home. Catherine had been totally unprepared for the miles of parkland, the exquisitely laid out gardens, and the magnificence of the house. Her grandfather's home at Newlands was simply a larger version of Renwick Hall. For a girl raised on rain-washed gray stone and vast stretching moors, the elegance of the eighteenth-century masterpiece that was Barton Abbey was overpowering. Even the surrounding countryside through which they had driven seemed richer and more orderly than Northumberland. Fields were neatly outlined by rows of hedges and the lushness of the shrubbery gave testimony to the gentler climate. No harsh sweeping winds blew here all winter, as they did in her beloved north country. It was all very different from what she was accustomed to.

And her husband. After several days in his company, she knew as little about him as ever. He could be kind. He could be very amusing. The trip had been tiring, but not dull. He had seen to it that she was comfortable, and that she was entertained. But what he thought remained a mystery. They were indeed the strangers she had named them, and it seemed that he had no intention of changing that. Catherine was conscious of a flash of annoyance as she came to this conclusion and was forced to laugh at herself. After all, wasn't that exactly what she had wanted?

Several hours later, she was facing the object of her thoughts over the dinner table. "The estate is beautiful, my lord. I'd love to see more of it."

"I'm sure there is a horse in the stables suitable

for a lady. We can ride around tomorrow morning. There are a few things I had ordered attended to when I first came home, and I'd like to check them out."

Catherine's eyes flashed at that "suitable for a lady," but she held her tongue. "What things?"

"Oh, new roofs for some tenants' houses, repairs in flooring, some fencing, things like that. It might be a good chance for you to meet some of our tenants."

Catherine regarded him thoughtfully. He was dressed in evening clothes; a frilled shirt, white waistcoat, longtailed coat, knee breeches, and silk stockings. The thought struck her—and not for the first time—that his was a face with too many reticences. Was this marriage a disaster for him? Had he loved elsewhere and been forced to give it up? Was the violence she had experienced a real part of his nature, or was it only a result of too much wine? He had been at war for many years, and she had heard from her father of his reputation.

Following her thoughts, Catherine asked him abruptly, "How old are you, my lord?"

His eyes flickered at the unexpectedness of her question, but he answered readily enough. "Twenty-six."

Catherine was conscious of deep surprise. "Why, you must have been just a boy when you went to the Peninsula."

His face was unreadable. "I was seventeen. The same age you are now."

Her brows came together, but she spoke lightly. "It seems we both had to grow up quickly, my lord."

He smiled in appreciation of her tone. "It would seem so, my lady. Now, what time do you want to ride out tomorrow?"

"I don't want to ride out at all if it's to be on a 'horse suitable for a lady.' I have ridden since I was two years old, my lord, and hunted every summer in Scotland since I was six. Have them put my saddle on one of your horses, please."

Allandale looked at her measuringly. "Are you giving me orders, Catherine?"

Her eyes darkened and looked directly into the lighter ones of her husband. "If you refrain from condescending to me, my lord, I shall refrain from ordering you."

Allandale's face lit with laughter. "It's a deal," he said. A terrific yawn, which Catherine vainly tried to suppress, caused his amusement to deepen. "I'm sorry to bore you so dreadfully," he said sorrowfully.

"Not at all," Catherine said with dignity. "I am merely a little tired." Another yawn mercilessly interrupted her, and she looked with indignation at his grin of appreciation. With tears streaming down her face from the violence of the second yawn, she rose from the table. "Goodnight," she said severely into his unfeeling mirth, and left the room to retire for the night.

The next morning, Catherine awoke with the sun streaming in her windows. She stretched luxuriously and looked with satisfaction at her surroundings. The sunlight carressed the warm wood of the wainscoting and brought to life the pale colors of the upholstery prints. It was a very large room, beautifully furnished with Chippendale and Hepplewhite tables and chairs. But, Catherine decided, it lacked something. It looked unlived-in. "Wait till I've been here a few days," she promised the empty Chippendale table beside her bed. "According to Kate, the least problem with my bedroom at home was the fact that it looked unlived-in."

A discreet knock on the door announced the arrival of her morning cup of chocolate. Catherine asked the young maid, who was regarding her with open-eyed wonder, "What time is it, if you please?"

"Ten o'clock, my lady," the girl answered, bobbing a curtsy.

"Ten o'clock! Good grief, what a lazybones I am." Catherine sat bolt upright in bed and pulled off the ribbon that confined her hair. She was conscious of a feeling of annoyance that the girl gawked so, but charitably decided that she must be one of the village girls hired by Mrs. Challoncer.

Catherine was not unaware of her looks. She was far too intelligent not to know that she had been gifted with rare beauty and that people received great pleasure from looking at her. Her mother, who had been quite lovely herself, had instilled in Catherine the conviction that she really could not take credit for what she was not responsible. Consequently, she was quite unself-conscious about her beauty. She could accept a compliment with grace and ease, but unless someone called attention to her looks, she rarely thought about them. Ironically, probably only a woman who had her assurance of looking flawlessly beautiful whatever she was wearing or doing could be so free of concern about her appearance. So it honestly did not occur to her that Nancy the maid was stunned by her mistress's classic perfection.

"Just like a fairy princess, she is," Nancy breathed to her great friend Lizzie, the parlor maid. "And ever so nice and kind."

Unaware of the commotion she was causing in the servants' quarters, Catherine was on her belated way to the stables. Allandale watched her coming, an appreciative gleam in his eyes. The bright sun reflected off her fair hair, tied at the nape of her neck with a blue ribbon. The light brown silky mass hung to her waist, over a riding habit that showed unmistakable signs of hard use. She walked toward him, swift and shining in the sunlight. If it were not for the long fall of her hair, she might have been a boy, her stride was so lithe and free.

"I'm sorry, but I overslept," she apologized as she came abreast of him. "I do hope the horses haven't been kept standing."

Allandale's finely cut nostrils flared with appreciation. Her concern was so obviously for the horses, not for him. She smiled up at him, her clear-skinned young face reflecting her pleasure in the beauty of the morning and the prospect of her ride. Allandale felt a pang of remorse. She didn't look old enough to be out without her governess, let alone be facing the fact of imminent motherhood.

For her part, Catherine regarded him with approval. His riding breeches and boots were even more worn than hers. When the stable boy led out a lovely mare, wearing a sidesaddle, her approval was total. Mounted, she patted the mare's neck, then stared at the horse the groom was bringing for Allandale. He was not overly big, but every line of his beautifully proportioned body proclaimed his Arabian heritage. His coal-black coat gleamed in the sunlight. Catherine's eyes, huge with admiration, poured over him.

Allandale mounted, and the picture made by the slender, black-haired man on the finely-made horse with his midnight coat, was striking. Catherine's voice was unashamedly envious. "James, you lucky devil. He's gorgeous."

The horse moved under him restlessly. "I know," he said. "And he's itching for a run. Coming?" She nodded vigorously and the two moved off in unison. Allandale watched her from the corner of his eye. She sat poised and balanced in the saddle, her reins held firmly but with care for the delicacy of the mare's mouth. He let his stride lengthen from trot to canter, and she moved along with him, obviously as at home in the saddle as she was on the ground. In accord, they let their horses stretch into full gallop. Allandale purposely kept a step behind Catherine, to admire more fully her horsemanship. She rode with unconscious daring and swiftness, her shining hair streaming out behind her as she leaned forward over her horse's neck. Watching her, he felt himself infected by the brilliance of the day and the beauty of the girl beside him. They moved through the early autumn woods, their horses' hooves thudding on the broad path. The sun reflecting through the leaves threw patterns of brightness and shadow across their swiftly-moving forms.

Laughing with mutual pleasure, they slowed their horses to a walk. They moved in silence, each afraid to break the bond the ride had briefly forged between them. Catherine's eyes were drawn inexorably to the horse striding so smoothly beside hers. "What do you call him?" she asked finally.

He kept his eyes on the path before them, but smiled. "Sultan."

She was delighted. "Perfect! Where did you get him?"

"Ireland." As he spoke, they moved from beneath the trees onto an open, flat moor stretching out toward the sea. They walked the horses toward the broad, flat rocks that ran all along the cliff. There was a sharp wind blowing off the water with a salt tang in it. Allandale's hair blew off his forehead as they walked, their horses' hooves clinking on the rocks.

"This is my kind of country," Catherine said, rising a bit in her stirrups.

His pale, catlike eyes watched her. "How do you mean?"

She gestured toward the rough grass and rocky ledge. "Wild," she said, "and free. One can breathe in a place like this."

He pointed to a deep canyon in the cliff. "When I was a boy, I used to jump that on my pony." Catherine looked at the ugly crevice. Twenty feet below, the sea crashed on jagged rocks. With a wicked grin, she gathered her reins and spurred her horse over the rock toward the crevice. The mare cleared the gully with inches to spare. Two minutes later, Allandale was by her side as she galloped toward a fence in the distance. In the blaze of his face she saw mischief and laughter and delight. For the next ten minutes they jumped every fence, galloped under every branch, and leaped every ditch they could find. When they finally slowed their sweating horses, both were laughing. "A horse suitable for a lady, forsooth," he apologized. "It's a wonder you didn't boil me in oil."

Catherine shook her head in response. "Nonsense, I shouldn't contemplate anything so mundane as boiling in oil." Their horses moved along slowly down a narrow path to the shingle beach. They turned and walked along the edge of the water, the stiff breeze blowing their horses' manes. Catherine drew in a deep breath, filling her lungs with the sharp salt air. She realized, with deep surprise, that she was happy.

She turned and looked curiously at the man riding next to her. The wild delight of that crazy ride had surprised her. And, she realized, it was some spark in him that had set her off. His face at the moment was still, all the planes and angles clearly thrown into focus by the bright sunlight. Briefly, it had been the face of a boy. Now, its firmly-etched maturity belonged to someone far older than his actual years. But his mouth had lost its usual hardness, and his eyes, usually guarded by those improbably long lashes, were as clear and bright as the sea. His hands lay loose on the reins, and Catherine found herself admiring their strong beauty.

He turned and Catherine felt color stain her cheeks. "Is that Wales on the other side of the bay, my lord?" she said over her sudden confusion.

"Yes." He, too, looked across the water. "The Pembrooks are more than half Welsh, really, through marriages and whatnot."

Catherine nodded. "The Renwicks are the same. In fact, I think we're much more Scottish than English. It's funny, isn't it," she said musingly, "How important the sense of nationality is to one. If anyone ever suggested to my grandfather that he was English, and not Scottish, he'd have a stroke."

Allandale smiled. "I know. My oldest friend, Davy Aberfan, is Welsh, and many bloody noses did he deal out at school to anyone who didn't properly recognize that fact."

"I think it has something to do with roots," Catherine pursued the subject, a frown puckering her brow. "We all need to feel that we belong somewhere. It helps us to feel less lonely."

Allandale's eyes held an expression she didn't understand. "Well," she said to him with a smile, "your Welsh blood must account for the fact that you look so Celtic."

"Not really." His tone was curt and dismissive. "My mother was Irish. I look like her. I think the horses are rested now. Let's get moving, shall we?" Allandale's black leaped forward under sudden pressure, and Catherine was left to follow as she would.

Feeling snubbed and rebuffed, her mood of momentary joy was effectively quenched. Why was it, she thought, that every time the conversation threatened to get personal, he retreated. It was as though big signs warning Keep Out were posted all around him. Catherine, a naturally warm and spontaneous girl, was hurt and bewildered by his obvious desire to keep their relations totally impersonal. Yet there were moments, such as during that wild ride, when she felt somehow as though their minds and spirits were totally in tune.

Prosaically accepting the situation for the moment, Catherine caught him up. As the morning passed, it became obvious that though Allandale had been an absentee landlord, he was very much aware of the workings of his vast estate. For all his tenants he had a charming smile and a sympathetic ear. Catherine, born and reared on a country estate herself, was thoroughly appreciative of his care. Her own warmth and beauty made a visible impression on the tenants, and by the time husband and wife rode back to the main house they were once more in pleasant accord.

After lunch, Catherine, drawn as though by a magnet, found herself at the piano in the drawing room. Tentatively, she ran through a few exercises and found much what she had feared. The piano was dreadfully out of tune. Going upstairs, she fetched a few tools from her room; then, rolling up the sleeves of her muslin frock, she opened the piano and began the painstaking job of tuning it. Allandale came in some time later, just as she was finishing.

"What on earth are you doing?" he asked, looking in surprise at her dirty hands and dusty clothes.

"Tuning the piano." Catherine had a smudge of dirt on her cheek as she turned toward him. "I hope you don't mind? I'm afraid it hasn't been used in years, but it really wasn't as bad as I was afraid it would be."

"My dear girl, why didn't you just tell me you wanted the piano tuned? I should have gotten someone to do it for you."

She smiled gratefully. "Thank you, James. But I haven't played in so long that I felt I just couldn't wait another moment."

He looked at her, an arrested expression in his eyes. "Do you play a great deal, Catherine?"

"Yes," she said simply. "And if you will excuse me, I'll wash up and sit down now for an hour or so."

"Certainly." Allandale moved off toward the library as she disappeared, but he left the door open. Presently the pure strains of Mozart reached his waiting ears. Unnoticed, his book closed in front of him. He sat perfectly still until the music was finished, then walked quietly to the door of the drawing room. Catherine was beginning a second piece and he stood and watched her profile from the door. She had no music in front of her. The second piece finished, Catherine rose from the piano and started as she saw him in the door.

"I should imagine you play frequently," Allandale's voice was expressionless. "You don't achieve that technical perfection without years of hard work."

She smiled. "You certainly don't. I usually practice several hours a day." Anxiously, "I do hope I don't disturb you, my lord?"

"No," he said, a harsh note in his voice. "You don't disturb me. If there is anything you want—music, or anything else—please let me know."

"Thank you, my lord," she faltered as the library door closed behind him.

V

To cause accord or to agree,
Two contraries in one degree,
And in one point, as seemth me,
To all man's wit, it cannot be,
It is impossibe.

—SIR THOMAS WYATT

Catherine sat on the beach and held her face up to the surprisingly warm October sun. She breathed deeply, savoring the tang of salt in the air. On impulse, she ripped off the ribbon confining her hair and shook out the single braid into a shining fall of sheer brown silk. The breeze from the water lifted the hair off her shoulders and blew it gently.

It had been the strangest two weeks, she thought. Perhaps the strangest thing about them was her own feelings. She had expected to be desperately unhappy, fearful, and homesick. Instead, she had an unaccountable feeling of—of what? She didn't quite know. All she knew was that she was not unhappy and, most peculiar of all, she did not want to go home.

Oh, she missed her father. She missed the familiar rough countryside where she had been born and bred. The neater, gentler landscape of Southern England would never exalt her the way the fells, dales, and rushing waters of her home did. But, for all that, she liked Barton Abbey. Running a large house was, after all, not all that different from running a smaller one. Instead of Kate she had Mrs. Challoncer, who had been the soul of helpfulness to her new, young mistress.

With a swift, beautiful gesture, Catherine stretched out her arms toward the sky. For over a week now she had had an indefinable feeling of expectation. What it was she was expecting she had no idea. But she felt as though she were poised on the edge of a great adventure. In some way she could not understand, this feeling was tied up with her husband.

Allandale. As her thoughts turned to him, her brow creased. She had every reason in the world to hate and fear him, but she didn't. She didn't at all. In fact, there was much about him she admired. His way with a horse, his responsibility toward his people, his sudden, blazing laughter, the way his long lashes lay on his . . . this is ridiculous, Catherine thought. You're in a fair way to totally forgetting how you got here in the first place. Certainly he can be kind when it suits him, and I suspect, she thought shrewdly, he feels a little sorry for me. As well he might! She shrugged, laughed, and got to her feet. Her ribbon was nowhere to be seen, so she simply tucked her hair behind her ears and made her way up the slope to where she had tied her mare.

Twenty minutes later, she arrived back in the stable yard, in time to coincide with the arrival of an old-fashioned chaise. With a sinking heart, she watched the elderly woman who was being helped to the ground. This must be Allandale's famous Aunt Louisa. Resolutely swallowing the lump that had suddenly arisen in her throat, Catherine went forward.

"Lady Lothian. We have been hoping to see you. You must come into the house and let us make you comfortable. James is so anxious to see you."

The Countess of Lothian regarded her nephew's new wife in silence. Catherine's hair, windblown and loose, hung to her waist. Her riding clothes bore witness to the many hours she spent in the saddle. Her face was lightly tanned from a week of lovely autumn weather, and the gold tips of her lashes and the gold streaks in her hair were brighter than ever. She looked tousled, slightly dirty, and beautiful.

The Countess of Lothian was a striking figure in her own right. Over sixty, she retained the upright carriage of a far younger woman. Her strongly-marked features testified to her character. At the present moment, the Countess's formidable face looked grim. "You must be the new Lady Allandale." Her tone made it clear what she thought of Catherine's appearance.

Catherine smiled in apology. "Indeed I am, and I must say I'm extremely sorry to be making your acquaintance when I present such a disreputable appearance. Do let me bring you into the house, Lady Lothian, and we'll find James."

Lady Lothian allowed herself to fall into step with Catherine. "I must confess that James's letter dealt me a severe shock. I had no idea when last I saw him that he was contemplating matrimony."

"No, I don't imagine you did," Catherine answered, the bright color rushing to her cheeks. "It—it was rather a sudden thing, you see."

"It certainly was." Lady Lothian's tone left no doubt as to what she thought about sudden things like this.

"Oh, Challoncer," Catherine said to the man who opened the door. "As you see, Lady Lothian has come to stay. Will you ask Mrs. Challoncer to make sure her room is prepared, and bring us some tea in the green saloon."

"Certainly, my lady. May I say, it is a very great pleasure to see your ladyship again?"

Lady Lothian looked with approval at the old retainer. "You never change, Challoncer. And how is Mrs. Challoncer these days?"

"Very well, my lady. Very happy we are to have Lord Allandale home again."

Lady Lothian nodded dismissal and swept before Catherine into the green saloon. Catherine looked urgently at Challoncer and he responded with sympathy. "I will find Lord Allandale immediately, my lady."

She smiled at him gratefully and, screwing her courage to the sticking point, followed the lion into the den.

When Allandale arrived some ten minutes later, he found his wife and aunt seated on opposite sides of the tea table, regarding each other tentatively, like duelists who try to find their opponents' weak points before moving in for the kill.

"James!" Catherine looked at him in undisguised relief. "Is it not delightful, here is Lady Lothian come to pay us a visit." She looked so undelighted as she said this that Allandale's mouth twitched.

"Ah, Aunt Louisa," he smiled with lethal charm, "how good of you to answer my call of distress." He moved forward with the catlike grace that characterized his every movement, and kissed her hand.

"Yes, well I didn't come for that, my dear James. I came for an explanation of your conduct."

"Naturally." He turned to his wife and regarded her disheveled appearance with undisguised interest. "Catherine, my love, you look, as always, charming. Do you have a name for this particular mode? The wind-blown, perhaps?"

Catherine's chin came up and she stared at him. "No, I call it 'Dirty and Disheveled.' I have already begged Lady Lothian's pardon for my appearance and will now excuse myself to repair the damages. I am sure you are anxious for a private chat with your aunt, aren't you, dear James?" Catherine rose from her chair and bestowed a gracious smile on her husband and her husband's aunt. After inspecting the chair to see whether or not her skirt had left any stains, she stalked gracefully to the door. And closed it behind her none too gently.

Allandale had a glint of laughter in his eyes as he approached his aunt. "Have you been grilling poor Catherine, Aunt Louisa?"

"Certainly not." Lady Lothian settled herself more firmly in her chair. "I was simply asking your wife a few pertinent questions—such as, how did she come to be your wife in the first place?"

Allandale's expression was unreadable. "And what did she say?"

"She said that the circumstances were somewhat peculiar, and that you would explain it all. Well, James," her voice deepened, "I am waiting."

He sighed and came over to occupy the chair Catherine had recently vacated. "I think, Aunt, I shall have to tell you the whole story."

"Please do," she snapped. "That is what I have traveled all this distance to hear."

Fifteen minutes later, the Countess of Lothian was regarding her nephew with undisguised horror. "James, I wouldn't have believed you would have been capable of such a thing."

He bowed his head. "You unman me, Aunt Louisa."

As his aunt opened her mouth to deliver herself of an angry rejoinder, the door opened and Catherine reappeared. She had changed to a dress of fine cambric and her hair was pulled off her face and twisted into shining coils on the crown of her head. As she took a step into the room, Lady Lothian rose to greet her. "My poor child. James has told me the whole, and my heart goes out to you."

Startled, Catherine's eyes flew to Allandale's. His were cool and distant. "I felt it necessary, my dear, to inform Aunt Louisa of the whole. No blame can attach to you."

Catherine's eyes clung to his for one more minute before they sought Lady Lothian. "Does this mean you will help us, Lady Lothian?"

"Call me Aunt Louisa, my poor child. Of course I will help you. The grandchild of one of my oldest friends!"

Catherine was looking more and more bewildered. "I beg your pardon, Lady—Aunt Louisa. Your oldest friend?"

"James has just been telling me that Alexander Maxwell is your grandfather."

"Oh, he has, has he?" Catherine rounded on her

husband. "I hardly mentioned my grandfather to you!"

"I know you did," he said. "Your father was much more informative."

"Oh." Catherine's look was thoughtful. "I didn't know that."

"It doesn't signify." He thrust his hands into his pockets.

"It certainly does," Lady Lothian was indignant. "Alexander Maxwell's granddaughter to be treated in such a way! And by my own flesh and blood!"

Unaccountably, Catherine felt sorry for Allandale. "Well, Lady Lothian," she said with spirit, "There's no use in berating James for what is done. Happily, my grandfather knows nothing of the circumstances of our marriage. He must never know."

"Heavens no!" Lady Lothian was emphatic in agreement.

Catherine smiled at the old woman coaxingly, "Then, will you help us, Aunt Louisa? You can help to make things all right with grandpapa, and James says you can scotch any scandal our sudden marriage may occasion in the minds of others." Catherine sat down, this time next to Lady Lothian on the sofa. "What do you advise us to do?"

"Well, my poor child, the first thing is to get you to London and buy you some clothes." Her glance consigned Catherine's favorite dress to the trash. "Then, of course, I shall introduce you to society as the grandchild of my oldest friend and the wife of my nephew. No one will dare to question your credentials if I sponsor you." Her strongly-marked features softened a bit as she saw Catherine's anxious look. "Don't worry, my poor child, all will be well. In the meantime, I am going to my room—no, don't come with me—and will see you both at dinner."

The look of horror on Catherine's face was too much for Allandale's gravity. "You may think it funny, James," she informed his mirthful face, "but if she calls me 'my poor child' one more time, I shall hit her!"

VI

How safe, methinks, and strong, behind
These trees have I encamped my mind,
Where Beauty, aiming at the heart,
Bends in some tree its useless dart,
And where the world no certain shot
Can make, or me it toucheth not.

—ANDREW MARVELL

The arrival of the formidable Lady Lothian put a rift in the ordered serenity of Catherine's days. Painstakingly, she had been building a fabric of security around herself. The only disturbance in her life had been the strange mood of expectation she had been experiencing.

But what she had been expecting was definitely not Lady Lothian. With her arrival, the steadily increasing intimacy with Allandale, which was the cornerstone of Catherine's newly found security, was severely interrupted. For long moments out of the day, most often when they were out on horseback, but sometimes during quiet moments, too, such as when they sat reading together in the library, Catherine had felt very close to this stranger who was her husband. But now Lady Lothian was too often present, and the minutes of shared sensibility were greatly lessened.

This disruption of something that was rapidly becoming supremely important to her put Catherine's temper on edge. And Aunt Louisa didn't help in other ways. First, Catherine's wardrobe was gone through with a fine-tooth comb and found to be dowdy and childish. Her tan was evidently a disgrace and her penchant for riding alone without a groom, dangerous. When Aunt Louisa broke in on her piano session, scolding her for fatiguing herself by sitting upright for too long, Catherine's patience snapped.

"I don't wish to be rude, Aunt Louisa, but I must point out to you that I am neither stupid nor a child. I do not find playing the piano fatiguing, and I do not appreciate interruptions while I am practicing."

Aunt Louisa raised her eyebrows. "I beg your pardon, my dear."

Catherine inclined her head and waited for Aunt Louisa to go away. Which she did, a thoughtful look in her eyes.

Later that afternoon, as Catherine curled up on her bed with a book, Aunt Louisa knocked on her door. Catherine called for her to come in, and she entered slowly. "I hope I am not disturbing you, my dear child?"

Catherine looked a little apologetic. "I didn't mean to snap at you, Aunt Louisa."

"You were perfectly right to do so, my dear. When one gets to be my age, one has a tendency to order people around. Don't let me do it to you."

Catherine grinned. "Do you order James around, Aunt Louisa?"

The older woman took one on the upholstered chairs and lowered herself into it. "No one has ever had any success ordering that young man around, which is part of his problem." Aunt Louisa arranged herself comfortably in her chair and regarded Catherine seriously. "I would like to talk to you about James, Catherine."

Catherine sat bolt upright on her pillows, her loosely braided hair over one shoulder. "What do you mean, Aunt Louisa?"

"There seems to me to be a change in James, a very definite change."

"A—a change?" Catherine faltered.

"Yes, my dear." Aunt Louisa folded her hands in

her lap. "What do you know about James? What has he let you know?"

Catherine's tone was expressionless. "Very little, Aunt Louisa. He loves horses, he reads widely, he is a responsible landlord, he appreciates music."

"I see. Has he been drinking at all recently?"

"Aunt Louisa, I don't think I should discuss . . ."

"Nonsense, my dear. I worry about that boy. And I care about him. It breaks my heart to see him throwing his gifts to the four winds. And I hope that perhaps he has ceased to do so." She peered shrewdly at Catherine. "He hasn't been drinking, has he?"

"No."

"What is he doing, then?"

Catherine responded slowly, "What I said. He spends a lot of time with Mr. Edgecomb on estate matters. We ride, we read, we've gone fishing and boating. Just ordinary country things."

Lady Lothian was looking at Catherine with satisfaction. "No, my dear child. One thing in all this is very extraordinary, for James. You spoke of 'we.' Nobody has ever dared to do that."

Catherine flushed. "Aunt Louisa, if I have inadvertently been giving you an image of marital bliss, I am sorry. James is everything that is kind, but we are not, we are not . . ." she faltered, trying to find words.

"I understand exactly," Lady Lothian responded. Catherine regarded her doubtfully. "Will you let me tell you a little about the James that I know, my dear?"

Catherine's eyes were steady on hers. "Yes, I should like that."

"Good." Lady Lothian leaned back in her chair. "My brother, James's father," she began, "was a very difficult man. James's failings can largely be laid at his doorstep. When Eileen died—but I am getting ahead of myself. Has James ever spoken of his mother?"

Catherine shook her head. "He only told me that she was Irish; then he shut up like a clam."

"I know," Aunt Louisa sighed. "James adored his mother. She was warm, and gay, and lovely. There was a kind of a glow about Eileen, a genuine sympathetic interest in everything and everyone around her. She was the only person my brother ever loved, and her death was a disaster for him. And for James."

"How did she die, Aunt Louisa?"

"In childbirth. The child died, also. James was five."

Catherine's head was bowed. "How tragic."

"It certainly became a tragedy. My brother drew back into himself and would let no one come near him. Worst of all, he insisted on getting rid of James's Irish nanny, who had been with him since birth. So in one stroke he lost the two people who meant love and security to him."

"But why would Lord Allandale have done such a thing?" Catherine's voice was indignant.

"She reminded him of Eileen, and he couldn't bear it. Unfortunately, James also looks like his mother, and the sight of his son was painful to my brother. I begged him to let James come to me. To my sorrow, I have no children, and James had always a special place in my heart."

"He wouldn't agree?"

"No." Aunt Louisa slowly shook her head. "Robert was a man who knew what was right, and it was right that his son and heir be reared at Barton Abbey. But it wasn't right for James."

Catherine had tears in her eyes. "Poor little boy."

"Poor little boy, indeed. To ask a child to live with justice, but no love . . . well, you can imagine how terrible it was." Aunt Louisa looked at her hands. "It broke my heart to see that happy, bright, charming little boy become the watchful, guarded, solitary man he is today."

"Oh no," Catherine interrupted. "It isn't as bad as that!"

"After all, my dear, it may not be. I have hopes, anyway." With that, Aunt Louisa rose from her chair. "Perhaps you are the very thing he needs."

Catherine shook her head. "I don't know about that. Aunt Louisa," Catherine spoke suddenly as the older woman reached out her hand for the door, "did James's mother play the piano?"

"Yes she did, my dear. Beautifully. I gave James some lessons one holiday he spent at Carfrae. He has an extraordinary musical talent, himself. But, of course, my brother soon put a stop to that. I will see you at dinner, my dear child." And Lady Lothian closed the door behind her.

Catherine slowly slid into a reclining position on the bed, her mind in a whirl. Obviously, Aunt Louisa thought that James cherished some hidden feelings for her. But he didn't. Catherine was almost sure that all he felt for her was regret and a concern to set her right in the eyes of the world. But Aunt Louisa was right in one way, he did seem at loose ends. She had never questioned her father's leading the kind of life she had described to Lady Lothian, but somehow it had always seemed to her as though James were simply filling in time. There was about him a sense of leashed power that made the pleasant country pursuits with which she had hitherto filled her life seem essentially trivial. Catherine's last thoughts as she slid into sleep were, "I mustn't fall in love with him. It could only mean heartbreak."

Meanwhile, the subject of her thoughts was reading a letter that had just arrived. It was from Lord Castlereagh, His Majesty's foreign minister.

My dear Allandale: I wish you would reconsider your answer to me of a few months ago. The official staff of the foreign office is rudimentary, and, to be kind, not really competent. We are in desperate need of a man like you. . . .

Allandale's eyes stopped reading at this point, and he tore the letter up. He sat down at his desk and penned a brief reply, then left the room abruptly and went to the stables. Fifteen minutes later, he was galloping along the cliffs. He turned his horse's head down a steep incline, and minutes later clattered onto the shingle beach. As the elegant black horse picked his way along the beach, Allandale's mind fell into a familiar groove.

That bloody Castlereagh. He had no idea what he was getting into with his brilliant notion of periodic congresses among the Great Powers in order to discuss the affairs of Europe. Russia, Austria, and Prussia were autocratic monoliths. They were interested in protecting their own monarchies and crushing any spirit of independence that might rise against them. Allandale was bitterly angry at the English government, but he recognized its essential superiority to the oppression represented by the other three Great Powers. It was folly for the United Kingdom, which stood for constitutional monarchy as opposed to absolutism, to think it could ally itself with the policies of Austria, Russia, and Prussia. "Castlereagh is going to come to grief over this," thought Allandale. "And I'm damned if I'm the one to pull him out." He ran his fingers through his hair and looked out across the water. The familiar bleak feeling of uselessness came over him, and his finely drawn brows came together. "I think I'll go home," he thought vaguely, as he turned his horse back up the beach. And stopped in surprise at his own impulse. By home, he had meant Catherine. He rubbed his hand across his eyes as he confronted this fact. He was becoming too dependent on Catherine's company. Somehow, she made him feel less restless, less alone.

A note of warning sounded in his brain. For he *was* alone. That was the one indisputable fact of his life that he never questioned. It was the reason he was alive today and not buried in some unmarked Spanish grave. It didn't do to become dependent on anybody. To lose sight of that would be folly. Allandale glanced at the position of the sun and uttered an expletive in Spanish. He turned his horse's head toward Barton Abbey and headed back to dinner.

It was a wary young husband and wife who faced each other over dinner that night. Aunt Louisa, uneasily aware of the semi-hostile atmosphere, tried to lighten it by talking of London.

"I must take you to see Madame Alençon as soon as we arrive in town, my dear. She will do miracles for your wardrobe. And Jeannine's for hats."

"I hate hats," Catherine interrupted. "They always give me a headache."

"Catherine!" Aunt Louisa was scandalized. "Of course you must wear hats. It will be thought most peculiar if you don't."

"I *am* peculiar," Catherine insisted. The whole thought of London made her nervous, and she was inclined to be stubborn in response.

"Stop teasing her, Aunt Louisa," Allandale put in. "People will look with admiration, whatever she wears, as well you know. She may even set a mode."

Catherine smiled gratefully at her husband. "I don't mean to be a disgrace to you, Aunt Louisa. But can what one wears possibly be as important as all that?"

"Ah," Allandale smiled satirically. "You are in for a shock, my love. There are people in London who spend at least seventy percent of their time worrying over what they will wear. The other thirty percent of the time they spend dressing."

"No one ever accused you of that, James," Lady Lothian flashed.

"No, and what a success I was, Aunt." The look on Allandale's face was distinctly unpleasant.

Catherine was alarmed. "What do you mean, 'a success,' my lord?"

"James means, my dear, that he was disgracefully courted and fawned over. People I had thought better of, too—Augusta Thornton, for example. I don't know who was worse, the young ladies or their mamas. It was enough to make one sick."

Allandale grinned at this heartfelt reaction from his aunt. But Catherine was horrified. "Good grief, am I going to be faced with a collection of outraged females? What will I do? What will I say if someone, if someone . . ."

"Don't worry, my dear. No one will." Allandale's tone was dry. "Aunt Louisa will throw the mantle of her enormous consequence over us—and I must admit, Aunt, that in society your consequence *is* enormous. And to be honest, Catherine, once everyone sees you, they will be in no doubt as to why I married you."

Catherine's gray eyes looked straight into his, assessing the truth of what he was saying. Seeing only reassurance in his steady returning gaze, she sighed and bent her head to her dinner. "Well, I hope so, my lord," she answered somewhat mournfully. "I could wish, however, that you weren't quite the beau ideal of young maidenhood you seem to have been. It's going to be awkward enough without that."

Allandale's shout of laughter was her only response, for he turned and began to make conversation with his aunt. But inwardly he was deeply appreciative. Any other woman in the world would have made a scene over that compliment he had just paid her. Catherine had simply tried to discover if it was in fact an empty compliment, or a reality on which she could rely. It was going to be quite amusing to see how Catherine took to London—and London to Catherine.

Two days later, they started out. Catherine and Aunt Louisa rode in the chaise, Allandale riding alongside. The ladies took advantage of his absence to have a tête-à-tête.

"The baby is due in March, I gather," Aunt Louisa started rather abruptly.

Catherine bit her lip. "Yes, Aunt."

"Well, fortunately, you're tall and will probably carry well. I anticipate being able to get through the season until Christmas. You shall go back to Barton Abbey for the holidays, and remain there until the birth of the child." Aunt Louisa's tone was peremptory.

"I suppose so." Catherine was vague. "I must admit that the baby seemed more real to me before than he does now. That's strange, isn't it?"

"Not at all, my dear child." Aunt Louisa patted her hand. "You've had a lot to think of lately, that's all."

"Is there anyone in particular I should be aware of, Aunt Louisa?" Catherine asked urgently. "Any special, ah, special, friend of James's?"

"Well, my dear, there is David Aberfan. He is the closest thing to a friend James ever had. They were at Harrow together, you know, Mr. Aberfan is a member of Parliament for Wales. He has some post in the government, I think."

Catherine was frowning. "How did James do at school, Aunt Louisa?"

"Brilliantly, my dear. It broke my heart when he left Cambridge to go to the Peninsula. My brother was crazy to allow it—James was only seventeen at the time, you know. He inherited the title when he was twenty-two.

Catherine's mouth was compressed. "Are there any lady friends I shall have to watch out for, Aunt Louisa?"

"Well, Caroline Amberly won't be too pleased, I'm sure. But then," Aunt Louisa looked disdainful, "I shouldn't worry about her. Set your mind at rest, my love." With which masterly and impossible advice, Aunt Louisa closed her eyes and composed herself to rest.

VII

O! how much more doth beauty beauteous seem
By that sweet ornament which truth doth give.
                                    —WILLIAM SHAKESPEARE

"Dear Papa, I'm sorry I haven't written since we reached London, but things have been so busy. Aunt Louisa has been hauling me all over the place—to dressmakers, hatmakers, bootmakers. It was rather fun at first, but I'm heartily sick of it by now, I can assure you.

"The ball at which Aunt Louisa is to present me to society is in two days, and I must admit I'm nervous. James tells me that whenever I'm in doubt about what to say, I should merely raise my eyebrows a trifle and say 'Really' in a carefully neutral tone. I practiced doing it in front of my mirror and felt an ass. Oh well, I shall just have to rely on instinct, I guess.

"Now to the hard part—what did grandpapa say when you told him of my marriage? I live in daily fear of seeing him arrive on my doorstep to enact for me his King Lear role. I can almost hear him now: 'How sharper than a serpent's tooth it is to have a thankless child,' he would groan to Ian and me whenever we did something he disapproved of. I know you told me you'd take care of him, but how on earth did you explain it? The first summer I haven't spent with him since I was six years old, and I get married without telling him. He'll be absolutely furious.

"He will find it difficult to object too much to James,

I think. After all, he *is* an Earl, and he's rich (you should see his London house). Of course, he is English, which grandpapa won't like. But, after all, *you* are English and—come to think of it—so am I! Unfortunately, we both know that he had other marriage plans for me. Which brings me to the second hard question—have you seen Ian? How did he take the news?

"The one lucky thing is that James's Aunt Louisa is an old friend of grandpapa's—she loses ten years every time she mentions his name! Evidently they still keep in touch, so hopefully that relationship will smooth things a bit. She has written to grandpapa herself.

"I have sat down several times to write to both grandpapa and Ian, but I have never quite managed to pull it off. What can I say? I'm getting very nervous, Papa. Please write and tell me what has passed between you.

"Meanwhile, I am fine. I feel very well and am enjoying London. My love to you—and to Kate, of course.—Your loving daughter, Catherine."

Catherine was folding her letter when a step behind her announced Allandale's presence. She turned around and surveyed him with approval. He wore a dark blue coat, pale yellow pantaloons, and hessian boots so highly polished she could see her face in them. His ink-black hair had been recently cut, and was almost as glossy as his boots.

"I must say, James, you do look elegant," Catherine said in admiration. "I shall have to exert myself to do you justice."

Where she sat, the morning sun touched her hair with gold and burnished the pure, fine-textured skin of her face. He smiled, but said, "From what Aunt Louisa tells me, I should rather be concerned about doing *you* credit. How much did you spend for that ball dress?"

Catherine compressed her lips. "I did not spend a pound, my lord, as well you know. I told Aunt Louisa it was far too expensive, only to have it delivered here yesterday. As a gift, if you please." Catherine was really agitated. She jumped to her feet and circled the room. "A poor man could feed his family for years on what Aunt Louisa spent for that dress!"

"Well, my love, Aunt Louisa can well afford it." At the stubborn look still on her face, he continued, "And it gave her much pleasure to make you the gift. She never had a daughter, Catherine, and she is enjoying herself with you so. Be kind to her? Accept the dress." He touched her cheek and went to the door. "I'm going to White's for a while. Don't let Aunt Louisa tire you too much."

Catherine watched the door close behind him, a startled look on her face. What a puzzle James was. Who would have thought he would even be aware of an old lady's need, let alone go out of his way to plead for it. That was exactly why he had introduced the topic of the dress in the first place, to ask her not to make a scene and insist on returning it.

He could see Aunt Louisa's need for a child and relate it to *her*. Could he not see it in terms of himself? In a moment of clarity, Catherine realized that of course he saw it. He just could not respond to it. So he was asking her to. Catherine slowly returned to her writing table and picked up a pen to write a note of thanks to Aunt Louisa.

At dinner that evening, Allandale regarded his aunt in amusement. "Are you actually living here, Aunt Louisa, or just taking your meals with us?" Lady Lothian looked repressively at her nephew.

"Your humor is always appreciated, my dear boy. As you well know, I am dining here because dear Catherine and I still have many minor details to go over in preparation for the ball."

"Really?" he said provokingly. "Now what details remain at this late . . ."

"James," his wife broke in determinedly. "Aunt Louisa and I saw the most peculiar thing today while we were driving in the park. An absolutely enormous man, with shirt points so high he couldn't turn his head, was driving a curricle with a tiny dog seated next to him. I nearly fell out of the carriage, I stared so hard."

"You certainly did stare, my dear, as I believe I mentioned at the time."

"I know you did, Aunt Louisa, and I'm sorry. But anyone who voluntarily makes an a— a cake of himself like that is asking to be stared at."

Allandale grinned at her hastily suppressed comparison. "I take it the 'ass' you saw with the dog today is Freddy Happlethwaite."

Lady Lothian raised her eyebrows at his use of the word Catherine had discarded, but held her peace. "It was, indeed. If he were not quite the richest man in town, he would be laughed right off the pavements."

"Will he be at your ball, Aunt Louisa?"

"Well, of course I sent him an invitation, my dear child. He is seen everywhere, you know, and I believe I invited anyone who is anyone at all."

Allandale asked lazily, "Did you send a card to Caroline Amberly?"

Lady Lothian's eyes flashed. "Of course, I did not. If you think that I . . ."

"What I think, Aunt Louisa," Allandale's voice was precise, "is that if the purpose of this ball is to scotch any hints of scandal, then Lady Caroline had better not be excluded." His pale gray eyes met hers purposefully. After a moments' silence, Lady Lothian's angry glare softened.

"You're right. I'll send it in the morning."

Catherine sat statue-still, but her mind was not at rest. Who was this Caroline Amberly? She had heard the name mentioned along with James's several times since she came to London, always when people thought she wasn't listening. Was James in love with her? The thought brought a distinct pang, and she thankfully acquiesced in Aunt Louisa's suggestion that they retire and leave Allandale to his port.

On the evening of the ball there was a slight drizzle

falling, but that failed to dampen Aunt Louisa's spirits. Her house in Mount Street was brilliantly lit, the ballroom looking like a garden with all the flowers that had been brought in. Aunt Louisa had invited a few select persons to dinner first, among them Lady Jersey and Mrs. Drummond Burrell, patronesses of Almacks, London's most exclusive social club. Catherine had been seated between Lord Jersey and young Lord Thorpe, and had succeeded in charming both.

Now she stood at the top of the stairs, under a brilliant chandelier, greeting guests. All of London was there. Catherine found herself dazed by the splendor of the gowns and the sparkle of jewels. She felt the shrewd, knowing eyes upon her, and maintained her calm, gracious smile with effort. Finally, Aunt Louisa turned to her. "The dancing is about to begin, my dear. You've done your duty here for the evening. James?"

Allandale was at Catherine's elbow. "We are to have the honor of opening the ball, my dear." And taking her hand, he led her to the center of the floor. His hand on hers was warm and reassuring and his smile, encouraging. She was a lovely dancer, and Allandale danced as he did everything, with his own unmistakable, fluid grace.

Hundred of eyes were on them, and many smiled with pleasure at the picture they made. The man's black hair and dark coat made a striking contrast to his partner's fairness. Catherine's golden brown hair was worn simply—the result of another fight with Aunt Louisa. "I can't stand ringlets hanging about my face, Aunt! All I shall do is push at them all night. My hair is too straight to curl properly, anyway." She was right, Aunt Louisa thought, watching the young couple on the floor. Catherine's hair was worn in a high chignon; the only ornament setting off the purity of her face was a pair of pearl earrings. The long line of her throat was broken by a strand of perfectly matched pearls, an Allandale family heirloom James had presented to her that morning. Her dress of pale champagne lace, the subject of so much dispute due to its exorbitant cost,

completed a look of uncluttered, classic perfection. She
made every other woman in the room look fussy.

More and more couples came onto the floor and by
the end of the dance Catherine was really enjoying herself. As the music stopped, she looked up at Allandale,
a smile of sheer delight on her face. His eyes as he
looked at her held an expression she couldn't define
but, as he began to say something to her, another voice
broke in.

"Well, James, how nice to see you after such a long
time, and so many—ah—momentous occurrences."
The voice was clear and edged with anger. Catherine
turned and looked into the narrowed green eyes of
Lady Caroline Amberly. Catherine's own eyes widened
involuntarily. Lady Caroline was stunning. Magnificent
red hair, skin like cream, and eyes like emeralds, she
stared at Catherine with unmistakable hostility.

"Caroline," Allandale's tone was smooth. "We are
so glad you could come this evening. My dear," he
turned to Catherine, "may I present Lady Caroline
Amberly."

Catherine, glad to see she was taller by at least a
half-inch, smiled. "How do you do, Lady Caroline,"
she said in her clear, beautifully pitched voice.

Caroline Amberly stared at the fine-boned perfection
of Catherine's face, and turned to Allandale. "My con-
gratulations, James, on finding such a pearl. But sometimes, don't you think, Lady Allandale, pearls can
become dull and one longs for the excitement of a
more vibrant jewel."

Catherine regarded her with clear, considering eyes.
Raising her eyebrows a trifle, she replied "Really," in a
carefully neutral tone. Allandale started to laugh, and
Caroline Amberly turned and walked away. Allandale
turned to Catherine, his pale eyes lit with amusement.

"You are a constant delight to me, my love. However, I must go and do my duty by all the dowagers,
and relinquish you to the thundering hordes who are
waiting to dance with you."

"Did you see that, my dear?" Lady Jersey's keen

eyes had not missed the brief encounter between the Allandales and Lady Caroline. "Really, Caroline looks quite furious. Small wonder—she couldn't have expected the wife to look like that!"

"I wonder what the real story is behind that marriage, Sally?" Mrs. Burrell's tone was skeptical.

"I don't know," Lady Jersey replied, "and what's more, I don't care. If Louisa can countenance the girl, she must be all right." Lady Jersey's eyes followed Catherine as she waltzed with Lord Milforde. "She's a beauty, and she's got breeding, that's obvious. Besides," Lady Jersey's tone sank, "I'd approve of anyone who put Caroline Amberley's nose out of joint." Mrs. Burrell concurred.

Allandale was taking a brief respite from his social duties when a voice from behind him interrupted his thoughts. "James, you rip, so you're riveted at last." Allandale whirled, his delighted smile making him look much younger than usual.

"Davy, you devil! I thought you were still in Italy."

"Only got back this afternoon, James. And when I saw Lady Lothian's invitation, I couldn't resist. So here I am, travel-worn and weary, come to have a look at your wife." David Aberfan's words belied his looks. He was of Allandale's height, with smooth, dark brown hair, a baby-like complexion, and clear blue eyes. He looked like a poet and dreamer. In fact, he was a rising young politician and Allandale's oldest friend.

"How are things in Naples? Did you meet any lovely young things?" Allandale's tone was cynical.

"I didn't go to Italy for romance, James, as well you know. And let me tell you," Davy took a step closer, "There is going to be trouble in Italy. The south, in particular, is ripe for revolt. And if that goes, the rest will follow. Austria will be out for blood."

"Yes, well that is Austria's problem, isn't it Davy? When they annexed half of Italy at Vienna, they were only asking for trouble."

Davy looked exasperated. "No, it is not just Austria's problem, as well you know. That bloody Holy

Alliance of Czar Alexander's will go to work with a vengeance. The three despots of the east—Austria, Prussia, and Russia—will move in to crush any hint of rebellion. And," in his agitation Davy gripped Allandale's arm, "they will want us to go along with them."

Allandale looked at Davy's hand on his arm, then at Davy himself. "If Castlereagh is ass enough to get himself mixed up with that gang, let him take the consequences."

"But, dammit James, it's not just Castlereagh who will suffer! Britain might do something to stop the Holy Alliance if only the right men were in power."

Allandale's eyes were bleak. "I hope the right men do come into power, Davy. Your best bet from all I can see is Canning. But leave me out of it, my friend, just leave me out of the whole bloody mess."

Davy felt familiar frustration surge up as he studied the adamant face in front of him. Dammit, why was James so stubborn? Allandale suddenly smiled, and Davy felt himself relaxing. Tactfully, he changed the subject. "Well, don't keep me in suspense any longer. Where is she?"

"You haven't far to look. She's dancing with Angus Cardross."

Davy let out his breath in silent reverence. Catherine was standing under a chandelier waiting for the dance to begin. Her tall, slender body was poised in expectation of the music. She turned at something Mr. Cardress said, and the motion of her head, delicately balanced on her long neck, was indescribably lovely. Davy turned to his friend and looked at him searchingly. "Where did you find a beauty like that, James?"

Allandale's face was without expression, the long lashes veiling his eyes. "She is Lord Carberry's granddaughter. I met her in Scotland," he said, giving the version he, Aunt Louisa, and Catherine had decided on.

Davy tried a probe. "It must have been love at first sight," he questioned.

Allandale's reply was courteous but final. "Certainly,

what else? Come and drink a glass of wine with me to-morrow and tell me all about Wales."

David Aberfan knew a stone wall when he hit one. Smiling, he agreed. And did not ask the biggest question in his mind—but what of Caroline Amberly?

Lady Caroline was not enjoying the ball. She had drawn her own conclusions about Allandale's marriage, and the sight of Catherine had dealt them a severe shock . The fact that Catherine was obviously making a resounding hit, and the cat-that-just-swallowed-the-cream look on Lady Lothian's face, didn't help. Nor did the curious and ostensibly pitying glances she felt directed at herself.

Lady Caroline Amberly was the widow of a very rich and very old baronet. She was just thirty years of age, though she didn't look it. But she didn't look seventeen either, she thought viciously, studying Catherine's radiant face from a distance. Caroline was too well-connected and too rich to be unacceptable, but her reputation was not blameless. She had been discreet, though, until the advent of James Pembrook, Earl of Allandale, into her life. At first, she had been drawn by his looks: the shock of ink-black hair, the startling gray eyes so tantalizingly hard to read, that beautiful mouth. All that was sensuous in Caroline responded. He was young and, aside from some Spanish peasants, probably knew little of women. Caroline thought it would be amusing to teach him.

But things had not gone as she had planned. She had caught him, yes. She had the satisfaction of knowing that the most widely sought man in London was *her* lover. But, with growing fury, she realized that it was she who was behaving like an adolescent in first love, not him. He was becoming an obsession with her, and she was in the midst of plotting ways to get him to marry her when his curt note announcing that he already was married arrived.

The wild rage she had felt at that moment rose in her again as she watched Catherine on the dance floor. "Lady Caro, do let me get you something to drink."

She turned and saw the Marquis of Elton at her elbow. With a major effort of will, Caroline produced a dazzling smile and graciously accepted. She then danced every dance and made it quite plain to all who cared to observe that she was having a very good time, indeed.

As the last guest departed, Catherine's mouth split in a yawn that threatened to crack her face open. "A trifle weary, my love?" Allandale inquired solicitously.

"How truly perceptive you are, James," she replied sweetly. "Aunt Louisa, it was wonderful. Thank you!"

"Yes." Lady Lothian looked tired, but her cat-that-ate-the-cream-look had become more marked as the evening progressed. "It was the first ball of the season, and I doubt if any other will equal it. Everyone came."

"They did indeed, Aunt," Allandale's voice was warm. "I must take my example from Catherine and thank you also." He bent over and kissed her lightly on the cheek. "If you ladies will excuse me, I'll go see if the carriage is ready."

Aunt Louisa turned to Catherine, deep surprise on her face. "James hasn't kissed me since he was a small boy."

Catherine smiled at her warmly. "Just because James finds it difficult to show his feelings, Aunt Louisa, doesn't mean he hasn't got any. I am sure," she put her arm about the older woman's shoulders, "that he has always loved you dearly."

Aunt Louisa turned and looked into the young face so close to hers. "No, my dear. I think that for the first time in his life, James is discovering what it means to love someone. And because that is so, he is able to share some sort of affection with others as well."

Catherine shook her head in denial, but Aunt Louisa hushed her. "You are the best thing that ever happened to James, my dear child. Don't give up on him, please."

VIII

Therefore the love which us doth bind,
But fate so enviously debars,
Is the conjunction of the mind,
And opposition of the stars.

—ANDREW MARVELL

It was several weeks after the ball before Catherine found herself with a morning to herself and nothing to do. It was raining out, so she curled up in front of the fire in the room that had been given to her for a boudoir, or sitting room as she preferred to call it. But she found it difficult to keep her mind on her book.

Resting her head on the cushions, she stared into the fire and allowed her mind to go where it would. Since the ball, she had become one of the smashes of the season. Balls, Almacks, the opera, rides in the park—there were always dozens of men clamoring to escort her somewhere. Everyone else wanted to be near her, why didn't Allandale?

Oh, he took her places occasionally. But one dance and he disappeared. Catherine recognized his restlessness, his growing boredom. In fact, she shared it. This sort of life was fine for a short time, but who could stand a constant diet of dancing, gaming, and chatter, which is what people seemed to do in London. Catherine longed to return to the country, to the long rides and quiet evenings when it was just the two of them.

But, no. That wasn't what she wanted, either. Catherine frowned and forced herself to be honest. She wanted to feel close to Allandale. She wanted him to smile that warm, unshadowed smile when he saw her, she wanted to be able to share his thoughts and his . . . here her mind shied away as she thought of the separate rooms, they occupied. True to his promise, he had never tried to come near her like *that* again. For which Catherine was profoundly grateful. But she was beginning to feel that there was a connection between those separate rooms and the other distances between them. Perhaps if . . . No. No! Catherine thought in deep agitation, and determinedly picked up her book.

Allandale's thoughts were running along similar paths to Catherine's. He was finding it increasingly difficult to continue playing the role he had assigned to himself. The deadly boredom of social partying was broken only by occasional chats with Davy. And, of course, Catherine was never dull. Far from it. Living with her as husband and wife, yet not being able to touch her, was beginning to set his nerves on edge. She was so damned beautiful. But every time he wanted to reach out, to hold her, to touch her, something stopped him. Either it was what he had done to her already, or her look of fragile youth, or . . . Or, to be honest, it was his own feeling that she deserved something better than what he had to give her.

Allandale was not unaware of his own shortcomings. Position, money, friendship—these he could offer. But Catherine deserved love. And he had none of that to give to anyone. With a distinctly unpleasant expression on his face, Allandale entered his house.

He was holding a letter in his hand, a frown between his clearly defined brows, when Catherine entered the library. She jumped a little when she saw him. "Oh, James, you startled me! I thought you had gone out." She had a book in her hand, and went to replace it on the shelves.

Allandale refolded the letter and placed it in his pocket. "I had just come in, my love. Don't tell me you have nothing to do on this dreary morning."

She smiled and shook her head. "A little peace and

quiet is most welcome, believe me." On this note, the butler came to the door.

"My lady, this letter was just delivered to the door." Catherine reached out her hand for it, glanced at the writing, and turned pale.

"Thank you, Marley," she said faintly. As the butler left the room, Allandale guided Catherine to a chair and made her sit down. She read the letter, growing even whiter as she did so. Allandale frowned.

"What is it, Catherine?" he asked impatiently.

"It is a letter from my cousin Ian." Without warning, the color flooded back to her face. "He is in town and is coming to see me this afternoon."

His voice was clipped. "And why should seeing your cousin Ian be cause to upset you so?"

"Ian," her voice was hesitant, "Ian lives with my grandfather at Newlands. His father and my mother were brother and sister."

"All this family history is very interesting, of course, but it still fails to explain why the prospect of seeing him distresses you."

"Oh God," Catherine rose from her chair and walked about the room in agitation. "You have to understand about my grandfather, James. You see Ian has lived with grandpapa since he was nine and his parents were drowned in a boating accident. He is like a son to grandpapa. My mother was grandpapa's favorite child, and I look like her. Do you see?" Her gray eyes, dark with trouble, sought his.

"Are you saying that your grandfather had matrimonial plans for you and your cousin?"

She bit her lip. "Yes, that's it exactly. Ever since Mama died, I've spent my summers at Newlands. Ian and I," her voice trembled, "well, I was closer to Ian than to any other person in the world, except Papa. He was like my brother."

He looked at her bowed head, and his mouth set in lines distinctly grim. "I am so sorry to have ruined your romance with your cousin, Catherine."

Her head jerked up, her expression startled. "My romance? No, you don't understand, James. Yes, Ian wanted me to marry him, and grandpapa aided and abetted him. But I wasn't at all sure about it. That's why I decided to stay home last summer instead of going to Scotland." There was still trouble in the wide gray eyes that met his. "But Ian and grandpapa will both be furious about our marriage. I don't know what papa wrote to them, but," she looked down at her tensely clasped hands, "I don't look forward to meeting Ian this afternoon."

His voice was uninflected. "Would you like me to be there?"

Her face, as always, gave away her feelings. "Would you, James?"

"I shall make a point of it," he said.

So it was that Ian Maxwell met both his cousin and his cousin's husband. He hadn't thought much about what he expected Catherine's husband to look like, but it wasn't this. His blue eyes took in Allandale's elegant bones, Indian-dark hair, and startling, light gray eyes. His first impression of effetism was quickly replaced as he sensed the controlled power of the man facing him.

Catherine made the introductions. "I am very glad to meet you," Allandale said coolly, holding out his hand.

Ian hesitated perceptibly and Allandale's eyes raked his mercilessly. He saw a tall, handsome boy with hair so fair it was almost silver, and very blue eyes. The expression in those eyes as they met Allandale's could not be mistaken. "So it went as deep as that?" Allandale thought, as he stood firmly, his hand held out.

"How do you do, my lord?" Ian's voice was stiff. He turned away from Allandale immediately. "Cathy! As soon as we got Uncle Francis's letter, grandpapa sent me. What on earth did you mean, marrying like that, with no word . . ."

"Really, Maxwell," Allandale's voice was chill. "I cannot see that we need justify our marriage to you."

Ian looked as though he would like to strike Allandale. Then he turned to Catherine. She stood beside him as if, Ian thought with rage, she belonged there. His voice shaking, he said, "Your marriage, sir, came as quite a surprise to most of Cathy's family."

"Indeed?" Allandale's pleasant tone held something that made Ian ball his hands into fists. "Well, it came as a surprise to my family, too, you know. I might venture to say that even Catherine and I were somewhat startled, were we not my love?"

Catherine was beginning to feel like a piece of goods over which two merchants were haggling. But she seconded Allandale. "We certainly were. It was just— something that happened, wasn't it, James?"

Allandale took her hand. "My dear," he drawled, "if we can't explain it to ourselves, I am quite sure you will find it impossible to explain to anyone else. I suggest you don't try. Now, I am afraid I have an appointment." He lifted her hand to his lips. "Nice to meet you, Maxwell," He nodded briefly and left the room.

As the door closed behind him, he was aware of the turmoil of his own feelings. What was the matter with him? All he knew was that the sight of Ian Maxwell looking at Catherine in that way had made him unexpectedly angry. He had felt it imperative to show the boy who it was who possessed her. He looked back at the closed door once more, and resisted an impulse to return and order Catherine never to see Maxwell again. Shaking his head to clear it, he slowly left the house.

Ian had stood for a moment in silence looking at Catherine. He felt somewhat the way he used to feel after being chewed out by his tutor. He looked at her, his heart in his eyes, and said nothing.

Catherine took pity on him. "I know how you must feel, Ian, and I'm sorry. But really, you had no right to come here demanding explanations."

"No right!" His voice was choked. "When you know how I love you, have always loved you . . ."

Her face was full of pain. "Ian, I never, never meant

to hurt you like this. I love you, of course I love you, but as a brother . . ."

He swore and turned his back on her. Her own voice became severe.

"Listen to me, Ian Maxwell. I have said that I love you, and I do. This is the only kind of love I have to offer you. If you cannot accept that, then I will have to tell you never to see me again."

"Cathy!"

"I mean it, Ian. I am married. I married with my father's consent and the blessings of the church. I do not propose to discuss this with you any further. Would you like to stay for tea, or are you going?" She met his stormy eyes, her own steady as a rock.

"All right, Cathy." His voice gave away the effort his capitulation cost him. "Let's be friends. I'll be glad to stay for tea."

The warmth of her smile only caused the ache inside of him to grow more painful.

"My lady, the Earl of Allandale to see you," Caroline Amberly's butler announced. Caroline's suddenly still posture gave away her tension, but she replied composedly enough, "Please show him in."

A moment later, Allandale himself was in her room. She had waited and longed so for this moment that she was almost overwhelmed by his actual physical presence. He was more desirable than ever, with that hint of violence and leashed power behind a facade of civilization. Caroline nearly ruined her whole scene with her opening line, "James, how I have missed you."

"How very flattering, Caroline. But I am sure you managed to keep yourself tolerably well occupied." The remembered timbre of his voice sent shivers down her spine and caused her to bite her lip.

"I have been busy, but bored. I rather imagine the same could be said for you, James," she said shrewdly.

He raised an eyebrow in reply, but went directly to

his purpose. "You wrote you wanted to see me, Caroline. Something to do with my wife?"

She flushed with annoyance. "Come, James. Surely you can spare a few moments for idle chit-chat with an old friend?"

"Certainly, but then, Caroline, I can never remember when your chit-chat was idle. You always have a purpose, my pet. What is it this time?"

"Very well," her voice was sharp with anger. "I see that little milksop has really got her claws into you good. Better watch out, James! Kittens grow up to be cats, you know."

"What the hell are you talking about, Caroline?" The gray eyes were dark with anger.

"Oh, I only want to warn you, James, before you make a total fool of yourself over that girl, that she isn't the Miss Innocence she seems to be!"

"Indeed? And may I ask the source of your wisdom in regard to my wife?"

"I have friends in Scotland, James. There are some very interesting stories about your dear Catherine and her cousin Ian. Oh, stop, James! You're hurting me!"

But the strong fingers retained their painful grip on her wrist. "Listen, to me, Caroline," his voice was soft but full of meance. "If I hear that you are putting around stories about my wife, I will make you regret it very much. Do you hear me?"

Her green eyes met his pitiless gray stare defiantly. "I hear you, James."

"Good." Her wrist was released and angrily she began to rub it. He turned to the door. "Whatever was between you and me is over, Caroline. Forget it, and busy yourself elsewhere." As the sound of his receding steps came to her ears, Caroline Amberly threw up her head.

"Finished? Don't bet on it, my lord!"

As Allandale entered his house for the second time that day, the sound of the piano reached his ears. He had by now realized that music was a clear indication of Catherine's mood, and a frown grew between his brows as he listened to the cacophony of sound that poured from the drawing room. He entered and stood at the door until the piece was over. "What has happened to distress you, Catherine?" he asked quietly.

She turned around, almost as if she had expected him to be there. "Oh, James, I just feel so badly about Ian, that's all."

He looked grim. "Did he give you a hard time after I left?"

She shook her head. "No, but it hurts me to see how I've hurt him." She walked to the window and stood with her back to him. "I think it must be the worst thing in the world," she said softly, "to hurt someone you love."

His voice was harsh. "It was not your fault."

She sighed and turned around to face him. "But it is," she said. "I love Ian. We share a common childhood—surely one of the strongest of bonds. I knew him as I know few other people. But I never would have married him. So you see," she smiled wistfully, "I would have hurt him eventually in any case."

She seated herself on the piano bench again and spoke with difficulty. "You must understand, James, that whatever our forced marriage may have destroyed for you, no hopes of mine were broken."

As he so often did, he knew exactly what she was saying to him. "Believe me, my love, no plans of mine were altered by our marriage." Her wide, searching gaze met and held his. He came closer until he stood over her. "Caroline Amberly was a whim that has passed. You are not to concern yourself with her."

Her eyes fell, and he reached out a finger and placed it under her chin. "Do you hear me?" he said gently.

Her smile was bewitching. "I hear you."

Involuntarily, his hand moved in a light caress across her cheek, Then he stepped back. "I'll leave you to Mozart, Catherine. Don't worry about young Ian. He'll survive."

Two mornings later, Catherine was devoting herself to domestic affairs. She had on a loose dress of pale yellow wool and her hair was held off her face by a simple yellow ribbon. Aunt Louisa deplored Catherine's penchant for going around the house with her hair down, but Catherine insisted it was important to let one's hair rest occasionally. Looking at her shining, silky tresses, Aunt Louisa had to agree that it certainly seemed to work.

Having interviewed the cook, Catherine was in the main hall on her way to see the housekeeper when her attention was attracted by an open window in the library. The curtains were blowing strongly and she looked in to see if Allandale was there. Some documents and letters were on the desk, in danger of blowing off, so she went over to close the window. As she turned back into the room, she noticed one of the bookcases appeared to be pulled out from the wall. Going to investigate, she saw that the bookcase concealed what was a small closet, seemingly a safe of some sort. Intrigued, she stepped forward, touching the edge of the bookcase as she did so. Immediately, the case swung shut behind her, trapping her in the tiny, dark room.

Catherine stood still for a moment, paralyzed by surprise. Then, as she tried to push the door open, and failed, a familiar panic began to wash over her. Frantically she pushed on the door, as the nightmare of suffocation and entrapment engulfed her. Stark terror took possession of her, and she began to beat hysterically on the door. Her breath stuck painfully in her throat as she struggled to breathe. Her hands hurt, but still she crashed them again and again as she sobbed "Let me out! Please, please, let me out!" After what seemed like hours but was in fact only minutes, the door opened and she fell into Allandale's arms.

"Catherine. What happened?" He heard with alarm her labored breathing and felt the uncontrolled shaking of her body. "Sh, sh, it's all right. Come on now, love. You're all right now." His voice was gentle, his arms comforting, and soon Catherine began to quiet. He led her slowly to a chair and made her sit down. Distress was clear on his face as he took in her white face, streaming hair, and bloody hands.

Catherine made an heroic effort to control herself, and with trembling voice told him how she came to be trapped. He deliberately pitched his voice at a calm, even, everyday level, as he recounted to her the story of how his grandfather had caused the compartment to be built. "I only use it now for important documents, like my will," he concluded.

Catherine had used the respite he gave her to advantage. Her breathing had slowed, and she was in control of herself once more. Haltingly, she began to explain to him why it was she had panicked so badly. "I can't seem to help it, James. I feel as though I'm suffocating, even though I guess I know I'm not. It's as though a big black cloud has settled on all my rational faculties, and I just totally panic." Her lip trembled. "I feel such a fool."

Allandale gently smoothed the hair off her face. "Don't be silly, my love. It's not all that uncommon a fear, you know. If it happens again, I suggest you try to focus on one thought and keep it in your mind. If you bring all your attention to bear on one thing, you might hold back the panic. And now, I think you ought to lie down for a while."

Catherine nodded wanly. "I think I will." She turned at the door and looked back at him soberly. "Thank you, James." He sat for some time looking at the closet where Catherine had been caught, his eyes dark with thought.

Catherine appeared to be recovered at dinner that evening, and went with Aunt Louisa to Almacks seemingly in very good spirits. At the last minute, Allandale decided to accompany them. He spent most of the evening in the refreshment room, where he ran into someone he had met briefly in the Peninsula. Forced to listen to the man's stupid reminiscences, he left to escort his wife and aunt home in very bad temper. Alone in the coach with Catherine after leaving Aunt Louisa off in Mount Street, he asked how she was feeling.

"Fine, James, thank you." There was a pause, then, tentatively, she began, "But I fear something has occurred to upset you."

He was on the verge of giving her a curt answer, but stopped himself. After a moment, he gave way to his impulse and answered her truthfully. "I ran into John Martinson at Almacks. He insisted on re-fighting every battle of the war over again, and wound up putting me into a temper. I'm afraid I was very rude to him."

Catherine gazed carefully at her hands. "It must be very difficult," she said, "to have to listen to someone going on and on about something they really know nothing about."

He looked at her sharply. "Martinson was in the Peninsula, Catherine."

"Yes, I gathered that," she said. "But he was with Wellington, wasn't he? He wasn't in Spain with you?"

"No." His voice was abrupt.

"Once," Catherine said musingly, "when we were studying the wars of Robert Bruce, Papa said to me, 'A guerrilla war fought by a largely civilian population is the most brutal, pitiless thing in the world.' But men like Martinson didn't see your war, James. They can forget the ugliness and remember only the glory." She turned to find him looking at her. The darkness hid the expression in his eyes, but his voice gave his feelings away.

"I would like very much to further my acquaintance with your papa, Catherine."

She smiled at him delightedly. "I'm sure Papa would like that too, James."

Catherine fought through the blackness and the suffocation. Dimly, as the walls closed in on her, she heard James's voice. "Catherine, Catherine!" She woke abruptly, bathed in sweat in the cold night, her breath whistling hoarsely in her throat. She sat up in bed, trembling with remembered fear, and her eyes slowly focused on Allandale's concerned face. "Catherine," he repeated. "Wake up. It's all right."

"Oh!" With a sudden movement, Catherine flung herself into his arms. "It was the dream, James. I thought it had gone away again."

"Hush." His arms held her comfortingly. "What dream, my love?"

In a trembling voice, she told him about her private nightmare. "It must have been this afternoon that triggered it," she concluded, looking up at him with dark eyes, where traces of fear still lurked.

He smiled at her reassuringly. "Well, it's all right now. See," he pointed to his candle on the table, "there is a light, and you are safe in your own room."

She looked around and heaved a sigh of relief, then nestled more snugly into his arms. "Yes," her voice was muffled, "I feel safer now."

Allandale looked down at the silky, brown head buried in his chest, and his mouth took on a set look. He could feel the warmth of her skin through the lawn of her nightgown. The nape of her neck was revealed where her long brown braid had fallen forward across her shoulder. He wanted nothing more than to hide his face in its smoothness, to kiss away her fear and bury it with passion.

Carefully, he put her from him. "You'll be all right, now, I think, Catherine." His voice was harsh.

She sensed his withdrawal, in mind as well as body, and sought to find the reason. He was in his shirt and breeches. The shirt was open at the neck and nearly unbuttoned. Evidently, he had been undressing for bed when he heard her call out in her sleep. She looked in wonder at the strong, smooth column of his neck, the strongly muscled chest revealed by the candlelight. An unfamiliar feeling stirred within her and to hide it she smiled uncertainly. "It seems I am always thanking you for coming to my rescue."

He was curt. "You don't have to thank me for anything." He walked to the door. "Goodnight, Catherine. Sleep well."

Catherine was left staring at the closed door, a frown between her delicate brows.

IX

My God, what is a heart?
Silver, or gold, or precious stone,
Or star, or rainbow, or a part
Of all these things, or all of them in one?

—GEORGE HERBERT

"Dear Papa," wrote Catherine. "I hope very much you will join us at Barton Abbey for Christmas. I miss you very much, and I think you and James would like each other if you met under different circumstances.

"I told you Ian had come to town. I've seen quite a bit of him, but I must admit, I'm not finding his company exactly enjoyable. He looks so unhappy and it makes me feel so guilty! I've tried to introduce him to some pretty girls, but he isn't interested. All he wants to do is mope around after me, looking mournful. He's driving me distracted. And James doesn't like it at all. I can't wait until Christmas and he goes home to Scotland.

"Speaking of Scotland, I finally heard from Grandpapa. He ranted and raved ('How sharper than a serpent's tooth,' etc.), but you and Aunt Louisa must have told him a good story. At any rate, he told me to bring James to Newlands, which was more than I expected. I rather thought I'd be told never to darken his door again.

"Darling Papa, do come to Somerset for Christmas. Lady Lothian will be there, and I'm sure you will like her very much. She remembers Mams from when she was a little girl! Write soon and let me know.—Your loving daughter, Catherine."

Catherine put down her pen and turned in her chair as she heard Allandale's voice in the hall. She folded her letter carefully and went to the door, meaning to ask him to frank it for her. She stopped abruptly and an involuntary, sharp intake of breath gave away her presence as she saw who was in the hall with Allandale.

Captain Matthew Armstrong was almost as disconcerted as she. Watching the blood drain from her face, he turned in some agitation to Allandale. Allandale's face was expressionless and he introduced them as though they were strangers. After they had mumbled restrained greetings to each other, he continued pleasantly, "Captain Armstrong and I are going out for the evening, my dear. I won't be dining with you, after all."

Catherine nodded. "Have a pleasant evening," she said faintly, and escaped up the stairs to her sitting room.

What was that awful man doing here, Catherine thought fearfully. Somehow her mind had managed to assign all the blame for that dreadful evening in July to Matt Armstrong. Clearly, he was an evil influence on Allandale. Inciting him to drink and violence. Catherine shivered and hoped he would disappear as suddenly as he had arrived.

Over a bottle of wine, Allandale looked with amused comprehension at Captain Armstrong. "But, Matt, what about your 'peaceful nest' in Scotland? If I recall correctly, you spent the whole time I was there regaling me with its perfection."

"Aye, Jamie lad, I know I did." Matt put down his glass and peered sheepishly at Allandale. "But the truth of it is, it's damn dull. Hunting and fishing are aye fine as a holiday, but they're no fun once they become the main business of your life." Matt looked gloomy. "God, after a while I didn't even know what day of the week it was."

Allandale was noncommittal. "And do you have a solution to this boredom Matt?"

"That I do, Jamie." Matt looked excitedly at the reserved face across the table from him. "I'm off to South America to fight with Bolívar."

"What?" The word leaped across the table at Matt.

"That's right laddie. And I have you to thank. Remember how you used to talk about him?"

"Yes."

Matt leaned closer and spoke persuasively. "Bolívar is gathering troops at Angostura, and he's going to push the bloody Spanish colonial system right off the map of South America. He's looking for men, Jamie." Then Matt played his final card. "Why don't you come with me?"

Allandale's lashes hid the expression in his eyes. "The Cartagena Memorial," he said musingly. "I've read it, of course. A brilliant analysis of why the revolution failed in Venezuela, and why she must win her freedom. He is a man worth following, Simón Bolívar."

Matt spoke softly. "Then why not come?"

Allandale looked at him fully, his brilliant eyes betraying the intensity of his feelings. "Get thee behind me, Satan," he said seriously. "Not because I don't want to, Matt, but because I can't."

"Why not?"

" 'He that hath wife and child hath given hostages to fortune,' " Allandale quoted. "You do remember that I've acquired a wife, Matt? I can't just turn my back on Catherine and take off to South America for years."

"Oh." Matt looked nonplussed. "I confess, I hadn't thought of that. But surely, lad, you're free to do what you want? You've given the lass your name. What more can she expect from you?"

Allandale's voice was pleasant, but the tautness of his mouth betrayed his anger. "She can expect that her husband does not desert her before the birth of her child, leaving her prey to all kinds of malicious gossip."

"But Jamie . . ." Matt began, only to be interrupted

by Allandale. His gray eyes were like ice and his voice warned Matt not to pursue the subject further.

"There is nothing more to be said, Matt." His pale gray eyes held Matt's challengingly. Matt sighed and dropped his gaze to the table.

"Well, the least you can do is buy me a drink before I'm off to liberate South America."

Allandale smiled. "Your nobility moves me deeply, Matt. I'll buy you as many drinks as you can hold."

Later that evening, Allandale made his way home on foot. As he walked slowly through the cold, deserted London street, he was conscious of the bitter longing in his soul. To go to South America with Matt! To get away from all the boredom and emptiness of his present daily round and throw his energies into something worth fighting for. His eyes blazed as he thought of it.

And what was holding him? A woman. An unjust and illogical anger smoldered in the depths of his mind against Catherine. If it were not for her, he would be on that boat in a week. Breathing deeply to clear the wine fumes from his brain, he reached the bottom of Grosvenor Square and headed toward his house.

Ian Maxwell was escorting Catherine home from Almacks when Allandale arrived at the doorstep. He halted on the pavement, surveying the scene before him. The lamplight shone on the fair hair of the tall man as he bent to say something to the girl. Catherine's hair was hidden by the velvet hood of her cloak, but her cameo-pure profile was clear as she smiled and responded. Suppressed anger boiled up inside Allandale. That bloody Maxwell again! With a decidedly ugly look in his eyes, Allandale moved purposefully up the stairs.

"May I ask, Maxwell," he spoke softly, "what you are doing with my wife at this time of the night?"

Startled by the veiled hostility of his tone, Catherine stared at him carefully. He had spoken quite clearly, only more slowly than usual. His movements were all perfectly controlled, perhaps too perfectly controlled, she thought, observing the brightness of his eyes in the lamplight. He's been drinking, she thought, with a sinking feeling in the pit of her stomach.

"Ian escorted me to Almacks, James," she said. "Since you were engaged," despite herself her voice took on a tinge of asperity, "someone had to take me."

Allandale's mouth set in ironic lines. "Here was Matt complaining that I'm wasting my life escorting my wife around town, and now my wife complains that I never take her anywhere." Anger underlay the irony in his voice, and Ian protectively moved a step nearer to Catherine, drawing a look from Allandale that made his fists clench.

Catherine looked at them both in exasperation. "I suggest we move inside, instead of conducting our conversation for the benefit of the neighborhood."

"Certainly, my dear." Allandale moved toward the door. "Goodnight, Maxwell." His tone was an insult.

"I'm coming in with you, Cathy." Ian's voice shook with anger.

Allandale's voice was like a whip. "Don't meddle in my affairs, Maxwell." He took a step closer to Ian, menace in his eyes. "And don't meddle with my wife."

Catherine was really alarmed. "Ian, for goodness sake, go!" As he hesitated, she gave him a small push. "You can come around tomorrow." His mouth set mulishly and he shook his head.

"I'm not leaving you alone with this bully."

"Ian!" Catherine's voice was sharp with anger, and she moved between the two men. "Go home, I beg you." He met her pleading eyes, and moved a step toward the stairs.

"Only if you really wish me to go, Cathy." She glanced over her shoulder at Allandale, and nodded urgently.

"I certainly do wish it."

"Very well," and Ian moved slowly along the street as Catherine rang the bell. The door opened, and he saw her precede Allandale into the house.

"My lord and lady," the butler seemed surprised to see them return together, and Catherine thankfully surmised that he hadn't heard the conversation on the doorstep.

"Yes, Marley. Coincidentally, we have arrived together." She turned to her husband, "I am rather tired, my lord. I shall go directly to bed."

He bowed to her carefully. "By all means, my love." As the butler moved away, he called, "Marley, bring a bottle of port to the library."

"James!" Catherine's voice was sharp with alarm.

The light eyes, turned on her, were empty. "I'm not ready to retire quite yet, my love. Can you think of something else I might do with my evening?" His lips thinned at her appalled silence. "I thought not. The wine, Marley." And he turned and walked away.

Furiously biting her lip to hold back the tears, Catherine ran upstairs to her bedroom. She dismissed the maid who was waiting to help her undress, and flung herself into a chair.

I knew it, I knew it, she thought furiously. That dreadful man! It's all his fault. But as the fire died down, she forced herself to face facts squarely. Matthew Armstrong had merely brought to the surface something she had sensed for a long time. James wasn't happy, and part of it had to do with her. She was his wife. Her hand touched the gently curving rotundity of her stomach. She was to have his child. But . . .

Tonight was the first time that Allandale had ever made reference to the fact that she slept alone. His hostility toward Ian had bewildered her, and she had been afraid of the fact that he had been drinking, so his sudden question found her totally unprepared.

She had felt fear tonight. Fear of what, she asked herself honestly. And the answer was blinding in its naked truth—she was afraid of losing him. His restlessness, his moods of late, and now the drinking. She felt him slipping away from her, and the thought was terrifying. All of a sudden it became perfectly plain that the one thing that mattered to her in this world was this man. She closed her eyes and remembered how it had felt when he held her in his arms. The blissful sense of comfort and security she had felt returned to overwhelm her now. She summoned up the pleasure she had always felt in his rare, careless carress. Slowly, the blight that evening in July had put upon Catherine's senses began to heal, and feelings she never dreamed of, like sensitive flowers, began to gently blossom.

Abruptly, she realized that the fire was out and she was freezing cold. With stiff fingers she undressed, and crawled into a cold bed. For the first time, she thought it would be nice to have someone there to warm her up.

Catherine didn't see Allandale until lunch the following day. He was pale and coldly polite; her few overtures of peace were met by an unyielding front of icy formality. By the time lunch was over, Catherine was nearly in tears.

As the days and weeks went by, things between them became even worse. Allandale ceased to make even a pretense of escorting Catherine anywhere. Where he spent his time, she didn't know. Her listening ear heard him come in at all hours of the morning. Obviously, he was drinking. It was as though a sheet of ice had sprung up between them, so that each could see the other's movements, but they were incapable of communicating through it.

Catherine wasn't the only one who was troubled by Allandale's behavior. Davy Aberfan watched his friend and felt perilously close to despair himself. He recognized that masklike look of total control and knew the emotions it was hiding. He stood at the edge of the gaming room of a very exclusive club one evening and watched Allandale as he dealt the cards. He was winning, and had been winning all evening, but from the empty expression in his eyes, Davy knew he hardly realized it.

"Damn," Lord George Bristol threw the cards on the table. "You've the devil's own luck, Allandale. I'm quitting while I still have my estates to call my own!" Allandale's eyes were hidden by his lashes.

"True," he said in an odd voice. "I'm a very lucky fellow, Bristol. You're wise not to stay in the same room with me." From the slow, carefully enunciated words, Davy realized that he was very drunk. He took two steps toward his friend and halted, as he was preceded by Lady Caroline Amberly. Caroline wore green velvet, which set off her eyes and magnificent white shoulders. Allandale rose carefully to his feet as she approached, then sat down again as she said something to him. She took the chair recently vacated by Lord George and, leaning forward, began to speak to Allandale, a pleading expression on her beautiful face. He looked back at her, amused cynicism the only expression Davy could discern.

Davy moved slowly to join them. "Breaking the bank, James?" he asked, nodding at the pile of guineas in front of Allandale. "Your servant, Lady Caroline."

Caroline's green eyes spit fire at the interruption, but she answered sweetly enough, "Lord Allandale has just volunteered to escort me home, as one of my horses appears to have injured a leg."

"Indeed?" Davy's whole expression bespoke his incredulity.

Allandale's Indian-black hair was disordered, his neckcloth loosened, but the gray eyes that regarded Davy were full of comprehension. And anger. He rose to his feet in a motion of controlled smoothness and took Caroline's arm. "I have always been susceptible, my dear, to beauty in distress." He spoke to Caroline, but his eyes were on his friend. "I shall be delighted to take you home."

She flashed a triumphant look at Davy and turned to leave the room. After a momentary pause, Allandale followed.

"Well, it seems as though our lovely Caroline has

got Allandale in her toils again." Davy turned to confront the narrow eyes of Lord George Bristol. "I wonder if I might be able to console his even more lovely wife?"

Davy's mouth thinned. He turned on his heel and left. Behind him he could hear Lord George's mocking laughter.

Dawn was breaking when Allandale entered his house on Grosvenor Square. Caroline had begged him to stay longer, but the wine was wearing off and he was beginning to feel disgusted with himself. He had sent his horses home from Caroline's and a walk in the cold morning air helped clear his head.

Caroline's words were still in his ears as he walked briskly through the London morning. "Stay with me, James. She can't give you what I can." Allandale shook his head to clear it further as he opened his front door. His mouth was set in hard lines as he mounted the stairs to his room. For the first time it was borne in on him that Caroline was sincere. Why the hell did I start that up again, he thought as he paused outside Catherine's door. I let Davy's obvious disapproval provoke me into something I want no part of.

His hand hovered briefly at Catherine's doorknob, and with a sudden decisive movement he opened her door and entered. He had been only too eager to escape Caroline's possessive embraces. He had never been able to tolerate sleeping with any woman. Once the sexual encounter was finished, Allandale's only impulse was to remove himself.

Yet he stood looking at his wife, oddly stirred. Catherine's silky brown hair was drawn into a single loose braid and lay nestled on her shoulder. She slept curled on her side, like a child. Allandale stood silently, watching the long, gold-tipped lashes on her cheek, the exquisite line of jaw and throat. He reached a hand tentatively toward her, then drew back as though stung. Shaking his head in anger, at both himself and her, he turned on his heel and left the room.

Davy Aberfan made a point of seeking out Allandale the next day. He was sitting in the library when Davy was announced, and Davy himself followed hard on the heels of Marley. Allandale greeted his old friend with a distinctly unpleasant expression on his face. "Will you stop playing the bloody nursemaid and leave me alone?" were his welcoming words.

Davy steeled himself for an unpleasant interview and sat down with determination. "If you would behave as a mature adult, I wouldn't feel the need to play nursemaid." Davy's mild eyes blazed. "What the hell is the matter with you, James, letting Caroline Amberly get her claws into you again? And—wait a minute!" Davy jumped from his seat and crossed to Allandale's desk. "What is this? A map of South America?"

Allandale's face looked like fine sculpture. His eyes were suddenly dark, but otherwise without expression. Davy recognized the signs and dug his nails into his palms, but he persisted. "I understand Matt Armstrong went to join Bolívar. Don't tell me you're planning to follow him?" Davy's voice took on a harsh note. "That would be one way to escape your responsibilities here, wouldn't it?"

Allandale rose and took a few steps toward Davy, his face still under rigid control. "What I will tell you Davy is this—I will have no more meddling in my affairs. You are my oldest friend. My only friend. That means something to me. Don't destroy that friendship by forcing yourself into things that don't concern you."

Davy took a deep breath. "James, it's because I am your friend that I must talk to you . . ." But Allandale had turned violently and left the room: Davy was left talking to empty air. He sank into a chair and covered his face with his hands. It was in this position that Catherine discovered him.

"Mr. Aberfan! I thought I just saw James . . ." She broke off in confusion as Davy rose slowly to his feet. A rueful smile played over his features.

"I'm afraid I put James into a temper, Lady Allandale. I must beg your pardon."

Catherine sighed and came further into the room. "I'm afraid James is running on a rather short fuse these days, Mr. Aberfan. It doesn't take much to set him off."

Davy looked carefully at Catherine. Her face had thinned out and the beautiful bone structure was more prominent than it had been. She wore a loose walking dress of fine green wool, which disguised any increased bulk in her figure. She looked fine-drawn and fatigued and Davy suddenly made up his mind.

"Lady Allandale," his voice was urgent, "may I talk to you about James? I think you're worried about him, too."

Catherine looked at him searchingly and slowly nodded. She moved to the desk and sat down. "Yes, I am, Mr. Aberfan. Do please sit down."

Davy followed the motion of her hand and resumed his chair. He began slowly, "I have tried to talk to James before—this was not my first attempt by any means—but to no avail. He has simply shut himself off from any possible course of action."

Catherine rubbed her hand along the back of her neck as though it hurt. "I know. He just aches inside, but he will let no one near to touch the wound."

Happy to find her so perceptive, Davy leaned forward. "It's a number of things, really. You see," he spoke slowly, "when James went to the Peninsula he had nothing to leave behind. His father," Davy's voice was eloquent of his feelings, "was a first-class bastard. James was glad to get away. And he found something really worth doing in Spain. I think everyone forgets how young James was when he was in Spain. Too young, really, to see what he saw."

"I know," Catherine spoke softly. "And, after the war was over, he came home to the same nothing he had left."

Davy nodded. "James is a man desperately in need of a commitment. He could do a brilliant job at the foreign office, if he'd only engage himself."

Catherine came to the heart of the problem. "And why won't he make that commitment, Mr. Aberfan?"

Davy was rueful. "He can't forgive us for Vienna."

Catherine bit her lip and stared at the fire. "He thinks it was a betrayal, you mean?"

"Yes." Davy looked at her directly. "Has he discussed it with you?"

"No. But I imagine he feels the same way I do, only far more violently." She looked at him indignantly. "The Peace of Vienna, Mr. Aberfan, neglected entirely the craving of the European peoples for nationality and for freedom. The populations of Poland, Belgium, Italy, and Germany were mere barter and counters in squabbles between alien sovereigns as they divided the spoils left by Napoleon's defeat."

Davy sighed. "You are absolutely right, Lady Allandale. And so is James. However, instead of repining ever what is done, we need to be prepared to stop the further attempts of Russian, Prussia, and Austria to destroy national sentiment."

"What do you want me to do, Mr. Aberfan?"

"Talk to James. Perhaps he'll listen to you. Canning is anxious to see him." Davy jumped up and started pacing the room. "James has the kind of brains and discipline we need. People talk to James. Probably because he always looks like he doesn't really want to listen. They think he's safe. And what's most important, he knows how to sort the trivial from the important and how to fit all the pieces together to make the whole picture." Davy was deadly serious. "We need him, Lady Allandale. And he needs us, I think."

Catherine's head was bent, her voice muffled. "If he wouldn't listen to you, Mr. Aberfan, I doubt if he'll listen to me." She looked up and he saw that tears glistened in her eyes. "But I'll try."

X

She loved me for the dangers I had passed,
And I loved her that she did pity them.

— WILLIAM SHAKESPEARE

Catherine's last interview with Ian before she left to spend Christmas at Barton Abbey was stormy. It was a bitterly cold afternoon. A driving rain had been falling all day long. She was sitting in front of the fire in her sitting room, keeping warm and reading a book, when she heard steps in the hall. At first she thought it was Allandale, but she realized in a moment it wasn't. She would know his step anywhere. Disappointment flooded her; he had left the house after breakfast and she had no idea where he was. She had hoped the vile weather would bring him home. He was home hardly at all of late.

So her finely arched brows were drawn in a frown of some distress when Ian came in. "I'm sorry to barge in on you, Cathy. I told your butler not to bother to announce me."

Forcing down her disappointment, she smiled at him. "I'm glad to see you, Ian. This kind of winter rain always depresses me."

He came further into the room, uncertainty on his handsome young face. Ian had determined to 'have it out' with Catherine. Had she been happily married, he told himself, he would have resigned himself and borne his loss with fortitude. But, it was as obvious to Ian as it was to the rest of London that this marriage was not

88

a happy one—for either party. Allandale's behavior made it perfectly clear that he didn't care a damn about his wife. And Catherine . . . when he finally spoke, Ian's voice had undercurrents of anger.

"You look so tired, Cathy."

She smiled and reached a hand up to rub the back of her neck. "I need a change from London, that's all. All of this partying can be very wearing."

His voice was tense. "Are you sure that's all it is?"

She looked at him more closely and what she saw caused her to sit up straighter in her chair. She would have to pay close attention in order to get through this interview safely. "I think so," she said carefully. "I'm a country girl at heart. You know that."

He rammed on. "Your husband doesn't have anything to do with it?"

She looked at her hands clasped tightly on her lap. "Indirectly, I suppose." She raised her eyes and looked at him again. "I am with child, Ian. Doubtless that has something to do with my obvious loss of looks."

He felt as though she had struck him. All the color drained from his fair face. "What did you say?" he asked huskily.

Her regard was steady. "I said that James and I are expecting a child."

"No." He spoke abruptly. "It can't be. I won't believe . . ." He broke off and looked at her again. Catherine's figure had always been reed-slim. Riding across the hills and moors of Scotland in a pair of his old riding breeches, she had looked more boy than girl. Now . . . her face had thinned out, yes. But he saw for the first time the fullness of her breasts, the quantity of material in the skirt that fell from her high waistline.

"Oh my God." He stared at her, appalled.

She strove for lightness. "It happens, you know, when one is married."

He came to where she was seated, and his hand went around her wrist like a vise. "Cathy, how could you? Don't you know that he cares nothing for you?

He drinks. He gambles. He runs around with his old mistress. In God's name, Cathy," his voice was a cry of anguish, "why? Why did you marry him?"

Catherine's own color had changed. But she retained her calm and looked at his hand on her wrist. "You are hurting me, Ian."

He dropped her wrist and flung away to the far side of the room. "I'd like to," he said. "I'd like to hurt you as much as you've hurt me."

Her features quivered at that. "God, Ian," she cried, "have you no pity? Everything you have said is true. James doesn't love me. I have hurt you terribly. But you left one thing out."

He turned. "What is that?"

"I love him."

He made a gesture of rejection. "I don't believe you."

"It is true. Why else would I have married him?"

He looked at her, the conflict in his emotions clearly visible on his face. "I don't know why," he said heavily. "But I sure as hell am going to find out." And he left her alone at last.

Catherine was remembering this disturbing scene as she listened idly to Aunt Louisa's chatter as the carriage brought them nearer and nearer to Barton Abbey. Finally brought to attention by Aunt Louisa's calling her name, she started and turned toward the older woman. "I beg your pardon, Aunt Louisa, I was woolgathering I guess."

Aunt Louisa looked at her worriedly. Catherine had a look of fragility about her that Aunt Louisa didn't like at all. "I think it's about time you got away from the racket of London, my dear child, and into the peace of the country. You are looking tired."

Catherine forced a smile. "These last few weeks have rather tired me out, I must confess. I shall be all right with a little rest."

Aunt Louisa peered at her shrewdly. "Are you worried about James, Catherine?" The girl's eyes flew to meet hers, and she nodded comprehendingly. "Oh, yes, I'm aware of his activities. What's bothering him?"

Catherine's head was bowed, her eyes fixed on her lap. "Oh, I think he's just bored, Aunt. A change of scene will do him good, too."

Aunt Louisa patted her hand. "I don't think James's problem is entirely boredom, my dear child. I think he is fighting a battle against his own emotions." Aunt Louisa smiled complacently. "And he is losing, I am glad to say."

Catherine looked at Aunt Louisa. Her gray eyes were dark and stormy. "I won't pretend I don't understand you, Aunt Louisa. But you are wrong."

But Lady Lothian shook her head. "I've seen how he looks at you when he thinks he's not being observed. You'll see, my dear," she predicted, "you'll see."

They had been at Barton Abbey two days when Sir Francis Renwick arrived. Catherine was at the piano when he was announced and he was barely into the room before she flung herself into his arms. "Papa!" Her voice was muffled by his shoulder. "I'm so glad to see you."

"And I to see you, Cathy." He held her away from him and scrutinized her closely. "How are you feeling, my dear?" he inquired solicitously.

She smiled brightly. "Fine, now that we're here. London was beginning to get me down." She linked her arm in his. "Shall I take you to your room, or do you want a glass of wine first?"

"A cup of tea would be just the thing, Cathy," he was beginning when the door opened and Allandale stood on the threshold.

"Catherine, what do you think . . . oh." He brought up short. "I beg your pardon, my love, I didn't know your father was here yet."

Catherine smiled at him a trifle nervously. "I'm glad you came in, James. Papa has just arrived."

Allandale came into the room, his hand extended. "How do you do, sir? Catherine and I are delighted you could spend Christmas with us."

Sir Francis responded civilly, and as they exchanged casual remarks, Catherine watched them both. In appearance they were so very different—Allandale, black-haired, taut as a spring, putting one forcibly in mind of a caged panther; and her father, tall, his dark blonde hair streaked with white, with the indefinable air of a scholar about him. They have at least one thing in common, Catherine thought, I love them both.

Christmas day was almost upon them and Catherine had still had no chance to talk to Allandale. He was polite to her father, casual to his aunt, and distant with her. Sir Francis treated his son-in-law with the same polite reserve he received.

The day before Christmas Eve saw a change in the relationship between Allandale and Sir Francis. It had been snowing lightly all day, and the whole house party had spent the day indoors. Sir Francis read, Aunt Louisa sewed, Catherine played the piano, and Allandale paced. After dinner, Sir Francis proposed a game of chess to his son-in-law and they went into the library.

Ten minutes later, he was staring at Allandale with speculation in his eyes. Sir Francis was an excellent player and had offered a game merely to while away the time. He had not expected much competition, and had played carelessly. He had been neatly checkmated.

"Let's play another," he proposed, setting up the pieces. The next game took an hour and a half and ended in a draw. His blue eyes alight, Sir Francis looked at his son-in-law with approval. "Do you know," he asked Allandale, "that I haven't lost a game of chess in ten years?"

Allandale grinned. "I can see why, sir."

"I underestimated you," Sir Francis confessed. "I had forgotten you were playing chess with real pieces in Spain. You must have been an excellent tactician."

Allandale looked appreciatively at the older man. "Knowing chess certainly helped," he said. "Now you, sir, could have outmaneuvered Wellington."

Sir Francis laughed. "I never told Cathy this, of course, but if I had been younger I would have gone over to Spain myself."

"Your secret is safe with me, sir."

"What really interests me about war," Sir Francis pursued musingly, "is not so much the skill by which men succeed, but the reason for their attempt in the first place. It is fascinating to see how some men begin with noble ideals and end up self-servers, while others take up a cause for basically selfish reasons and become transfigured by it."

Allandale's brows were drawn together. "Napoleon, I guess, is a prime example of the first category."

"Yes." Sir Francis looked up from the chess pieces. "The child of the revolution, sworn to liberty, equality, fraternity, ends up crowning himself Emperor and sees himself as conquerer of the world. On the other hand, you have a man like Robert Bruce, who started to pursue a kingship for himself and ended up devoting his life to winning freedom for a nation." After a moment's pause, Sir Francis went on. "I have never fought in war myself, but I think that it profoundly affects those who have. Either they become brutalized, thinking self-preservation and, eventually, self-aggrandizement, is the most important thing in life. Or they must find in a cause justification for the cruelty they have seen and experienced."

Allandale's mouth was twisted. "And what of those who find their cause only to have it cut from beneath their feet?"

Sir Francis rose and briefly rested a hand on Allandale's shoulder. "No cause is ever dead, my boy, as long as one person is willing to stand up for it. And, on that note of wisdom and inspiration, I am going to bed."

Allandale escorted the older man to the door and returned to his chair. For a long time he sat, staring into the fire.

Christmas Eve day dawned bright and sunny. The snow sparkled invitingly, and at breakfast Allandale said to Catherine, "Care to join me for a ride this morning, my love?"

Catherine's cheeks turned pink with pleasure. It was the first time Allandale had invited her to accompany him anywhere in weeks. "I'd love to, James." she said.

Aunt Louisa frowned alarmingly. "James, you don't mean to take this child out on a day like this! Suppose her horse slipped." As Catherine opened her mouth to protest, Aunt Louisa continued sternly. "I don't think Catherine should be riding at all. It is dangerous for her and for the child."

Allandale looked guilty. "I'm sorry, Catherine," he spoke with contrition. "I forgot."

"Forgot!" Aunt Louisa looked indignant. "How could you forget that your son is to be born in a few months time?"

Allandale looked at his aunt in exasperation.

"I'm sure a ride wouldn't harm me at all, Aunt Louisa," Catherine began determinedly.

"No," Allandale shook his head. "Aunt Louisa is right. You shouldn't be riding." As she began to argue, he rose from the table and gently flicked her cheek with his finger. "You must take care of yourself, Catherine." He turned to Aunt Louisa. "But how are you so sure it will be a boy?"

Aunt Louisa smiled at Catherine, then turned to answer Allandale. "I'm not. I'm just hoping."

"I don't know," Allandale said. "I rather think I'd like a girl."

He left both women gaping at him. "If that isn't just like James," Aunt Louisa said furiously. "And the worst part is—he probably means it!"

Catherine merely laughed.

Late that night, Catherine took her courage in her hands and went to Allandale. He was in the library, the fire casting a glow on his skin and causing his lashes to throw long shadows on his cheeks. She entered the room slowly and closed the door behind her. He looked up in surprise. Her hair had been brushed for the night and hung like heavy silk down her back. She wore a warm robe of burgundy velvet. She took a chair near the fire and spoke hardily. "I want to talk to you, James."

He was clearly startled by her appearance, the color at first receding from, then flooding back to his face. Surprise caused him to be abrupt. "What about, Catherine?"

She began obliquely. "I have been re-reading *Hamlet* lately."

He looked bewildered. "Yes, I've seen you with it. It's one of my favorites, too."

"I thought it might be. It's about a man whose whole vision of life is shattered by the betrayal and infidelity of his mother. Then he learns that his uncle has murdered the king—his father—and stolen his throne." She paused, then asked him briskly, "What does he do about it, James?"

Allandale was looking at her steadily. "Nothing."

"Precisely," she said. "Confronted by evil, he does nothing. He laments the state of the world—an 'unweeded garden' he calls it, 'things rank and gross in nature possess it merely.' He contemplates suicide. And what does all this bellyaching get him?"

"He got exactly what he wanted," Allandale spoke harshly. "Death."

"Yes, Hamlet was satisfied. But what," she leaned forward in her chair, "what of Denmark, James? He was a prince, he had a duty to his people. What did he do for them?"

Allandale rose from his chair and paced to the window. With his back to her, he said, "I hardly think this is the time of night to be discussing Hamlet."

"I wasn't discussing Hamlet," she returned. "And you know it."

He swung around to look at her. "I have no intention of discussing this subject with you, Catherine."

"No," she returned nastily, "I don't suppose you have the guts to." He looked at her, eyebrows raised in surprise. "You'd rather go on, hugging your grudges, counting over your feelings of ill-usage. If you don't watch out, James, there'll be nothing left of you except resentment."

His eyes began to burn with anger. "You don't know what the hell you're talking about."

"Oh yes I do," she snapped back. "James Pembrook feels personally betrayed by what the allies did at Vienna. The world didn't pay attention to his wishes, so like Achilles, he retired to his tent and sulked. Yes, James," she blazed as he made a motion of refutation, "sulked. 'If you won't play by my rules, then I'll take my football and go home.' Isn't that how it is?"

He was really angry now, and took a menacing step toward her. "I don't let anyone talk to me like this."

"Don't I know it. Everyone is afraid to talk to you. Your feelings, my lord, are more sensitive than an adolescent girl's!"

Allandale's eyes, black with fury, looked into hers. "You know nothing about it." A pulse was beating visibly in his temple. "You think *Hamlet* is a tragedy? It is not a tragedy to die when life is meaningless to you. Tragedy is giving your life for a cause, then having that cause spat and trampled on by those who profit from your sacrifice." His face haggard, he continued, "I'm not talking about myself. I still have my life, my health, my fortune. But what of the others?" His voice faltered momentarily, then regained strength. "Do you know who died in Spain? The best. Only the best volunteered for that struggle, and they were caught and tortured and died. It was too high a price, Catherine."

All pretense was gone, his face was naked in its emotion. "It was too high a price to pay for granting others the right to forget and betray what was achieved by the courage and sacrifice of a few."

She turned to hide her tears from him. Her voice remained steady as she asked. "And what of you, James? By refusing to pursue their dream as best you can through the medium available to you, are you not betraying them as well?"

In the face of his silence, she continued. "There are ways of exercising courage, James, outside of war. Committing oneself to a course of action, no matter how unpopular and difficult, is surely worthy of praise as well? What do you owe your allegiance to, my lord, yourself and your disappointments or the fallen cause of your friends?" She turned slowly, tears still glistening on her lashes. "Go to see Canning, James. He is no revolutionary, but he is sensible and he is the best hope we have to do something for Europe."

His mouth quivered and he buried his head in his hands. Catherine ached to reach out and touch him, but forced herself to slowly turn and move away. At the door she paused and quoted softly:

"While rolling rivers into the seas shall run.
And round the space of heaven the radiant sun;
While trees the mountain-tops with shades supply,
Your honor, name, and praise shall never die."

Allandale listened to the door close with the immortal words of Virgil still hanging in the air. Behind the shelter of his hand, his own lashes were wet. All the pain and guilt, repressed for so long, swept up to engulf him. With a violent motion, he lurched to his feet and flung open the windows. The icy December air shocked his senses and helped him to get himself under control. Slowly, he closed the window and went back to the fire. For a long time he stood staring into its dying flames, his mind filled with echoes from the past.

Pablo's face, young and trusting, then the broken body they had recovered from the French to bury. His own voice speaking to the governing council: " 'War is an ugly thing, but not the ugliest of things: the decayed and degraded state of moral and patriotic feeling which thinks nothing worth a war is worse. A man who has nothing which he cares about more than his personal safety is a miserable creature who has no chance of being free.' "

Then more recent voices intruded. "No cause is ever dead as long as one person is willing to stand up for it." And finally, "Who do you owe your allegiance to, yourself . . . or the fallen cause of your friends?"

With no one to observe him, Allandale didn't try to conceal the emotions that were rending him. Taking a deep and painful breath, he moved back to his desk and, picking up a pen, began a letter to Davy Aberfan. The letter concluded, he sealed and franked it and sat back again in his chair.

Catherine was right, he thought. She had held a mirror up before him and what was revealed he hadn't liked. But it was true. He had been sulking. An unwilling grin tugged at the corners of his mouth as he remembered how her eyes had blazed at him. She had succeeded where many people had failed; she had found the words to shock him out of his self-enclosed misery and into action.

Funny, Allandale thought, no one else in the world understands as she does. It must have been fate . . . then he stopped all thought as he realized where it was leading him. But emotion could not be stopped. Without volition, her face was before him. The long, straight, silky hair, the gold-tipped lashes framing eyes as changing and fascinating as the winter sea, the chiseled perfection of her lips, and delicacy of her throat . . . Allandale's breathing was hard and labored. My God, my God, he thought. For how long have I loved her?

He sat perfectly still while this fact, known by all his

instincts for months, rose slowly and took over his conscious mind. He hadn't refused to go to South America with Matt Armstrong because he owed anything to Catherine. Simply, he couldn't bear to leave her. And because he resented and feared this emotion, so alien to him, he had turned on her with anger. He left the library and paused before the grand piano in the drawing room. Slowly he sat down and picked out one or two notes. Out loud he said, "Catherine." By some fantastic stroke of luck he had found the one person in the world for him. Her clear judgment, her understanding, her laughter; he never had to explain to Catherine. She always knew what he meant, just as he always understood her.

Which meant? Did she feel the same way about him? He remembered her tears this evening as she relentlessly did what she had come to do. He looked at his hands on the piano, and realized that of course she loved him. The thing between them existed because it was mutual. She understood him precisely because she loved him.

He mounted the stairs and stopped outside her door. He tapped lightly and heard Catherine's soft, "Come in."

He set his candle down on a table and stood at the foot of her bed. Gray eyes, full of feeling, looked into gray. "I have just written to Davy," he said. "I asked him to make an appointment for me to see Canning."

She smiled. "I'm glad, James." The fullness of her emotions sounded in the aching beauty of her voice. Allandale felt a quiver run through him, but continued.

"You were right, I'm afraid. I have been a poor friend. Instead of bearing witness for what was right, I have been—sulking."

Catherine's gaze was clear. "You haven't been sulking, James. I just said that to try to shock you. But," her voice was very gentle, "you must stop feeling guilty for being alive. Guilt is a totally destructive emotion.

Dying in Spain wouldn't have solved anything. Perhaps you survived for a purpose."

He looked suddenly young and vulnerable. "My little Catherine," his voice had an odd laugh, "is there nothing that escapes you?" He moved toward her and gently reached out his hand to touch her hair. "Good night, my heart."

Catherine looked after him, a thoughtful expression on her young face. Suddenly, she broke into a radiant smile and snuggled down under the covers. "Aunt Louisa," she spoke softly, "I think perhaps you were right."

XI

What is our life? A play of passion.
—SIR WALTER RALEIGH

Catherine slept late on Christmas morning. It was the maid bringing her morning chocolate who finally stirred her from the best sleep she had known in weeks. She smiled at the maid, wished her a Merry Christmas, and settled back to her hot drink. For a moment she was hard put to recall why she had this feeling of warm joy; then she remembered last night and smiled blissfully. James had written to Davy and, Catherine thought, something of great moment had happened between them.

She decided to take a bath before dressing and instructed the maid to set up the tub before the fire in her dressing room. As she stood naked before the leaping flames, hair piled on her head, she looked down at her stomach, then walked across the room to the full-length mirror. She looked at herself sideways, and wondered how long it would be before her clothing would cease to conceal her growing rotundity. Gently she placed her hand on her stomach and felt the child move under it.

As Catherine soaked in the tub, kept hot by the maid's constant replenishing, it seemed to her that all the tension of the last few months was washed away in the water. She had not realized how on edge her nerves had been. She closed her eyes and softly sang, "I know where I'm going and I know who's going with me, I know who I love. . . ." She smiled secretly and said, "I think I'll get out now, Nancy." In a tunic of amber wool worn over an underdress of pure white, Catherine came downstairs on Christmas morning. Hopefully, she looked in the library and was rewarded by finding Allandale alone.

She peeked in at him, looking so much like a little girl full of Christmas expectation that he grinned. "Merry Christmas, my love." He kissed her on her smooth cheek and teased, "Are you by any chance in search of a present?"

Her whole face glowed. "I was more interested in giving one, my lord. I want you to stay right here, but turn your back to the door. Go on!" She gave him a gentle push, and he obeyed the pressure of her fingers. "Now don't move," she cautioned. "I shall be right back."

Obediently he stayed with his back to the door until he heard her come in again. "Don't turn around yet," she admonished and heard her moving a chair and putting something down. "All right—now!" Catherine instructed, and he turned and saw it.

Propped on a chair was a painting. Allandale was silent as he moved closer to study it. The anguish on the faces of the Spanish victims and the cruelty of the French soldiers was vividly depicted. It was a brilliant picture, full of pain and truth. "May 1808," Allandale said softly. "Goya?" She nodded. "How did you get it?"

"Papa got it for me," Catherine replied. "I wrote to him about two months ago, and he brought it with him."

Allandale made no attempt to hide his emotion from her. It was written in every angle of his face. That in itself, Catherine thought, was the best present he could give her. Yesterday, his lashes would have hidden his eyes, and the rigid mask of control stamped his features. Today, he looked fully at her and smiled. "You could have given me nothing that I should treasure more," he said, and even the timbre of his voice was different.

Catherine's own voice was soft with emotion. "I am so glad you like it, James." They stood for minutes in silence, looking at the painting before them. It was so intense in its representation of the horror of cruelty and the reality of hate and terror that they unconsciously moved closer to each other for comfort.

Allandale broke the silence as he turned to Catherine, the painful emotion in his eyes lightening. "I almost forgot your present." He went to his desk and out of the bottom drawer lifted an object and brought it to her. Catherine looked at it with awe and reached out her hand. She held the statue of a horse, some ten inches high. It was carved out of onyx and on the silver base was engraved her name, Catherine Pembrook, and the date. Catherine gazed at the horse, her face alight with pleasure. He stood on his hind legs, and the flaring nostrils and wild mane were all carved in splendid detail. Catherine looked again at her name on the base, the name that proclaimed their marriage.

Her smile to him was a felicity. "Thank you, James. He is perfect." The two pairs of gray eyes locked together and Allandale had taken a step toward her when there was a knock on the door. Aunt Louisa's voice sounded harshly in their ears.

"It's time to give the servants their presents." Allandale swore softly, but opened the door to let Catherine precede him out.

The afternoon passed for Catherine in a haze of anticipation. Afterward she recalled only Aunt Louisa's pleasure when Allandale asked her to be godmother to the coming child. After dinner, Allandale and Sir Francis accompanied the women back to the drawing room. "Play for us, Cathy," Sir Francis requested. Catherine smiled at her father and went to the piano.

"What would you like to hear, Papa?"

"Oh, some of the old songs, I think."

"Mama's songs?"

"Yes," he gave her a smile of great sweetness. "Do you remember the ballad your mother used to sing every Christmas? The one about the king of the faerie folk?"

"About how he lost his power over men on the night Christ was born?"

"That's the one." Sir Francis nodded contentedly.

"I never heard that ballad," Aunt Louisa said. "And I thought I knew them all."

"This one is more Celtic than Border ballad," Catherine said. "It tells how all the faeries were forced to flee to the hollows of the hills, and there they have remained ever since." She struck a note, lifted her pure young voice, and began to sing.

Sir Francis stared into the fire, the sound of his daughter's voice releasing a flood of memories. Aunt Louisa's eyes were on Sir Francis. Allandale, unobserved, was free to look at his wife.

Music always exalted Catherine, and the joy she felt was vibrant in her face. He looked at her and was swept by a flood of love and desire so intense it frightened him.

The last note died away and Catherine came back from the mysterious and exalted world she dwelt in with music. Her eyes focused again on the real world, and met Allandale's. What she saw there caused her to catch her breath. For a moment they remained thus, and the thing between them was so intense it stopped their very breathing.

Then Sir Francis broke it. A mixture of joy and pain in his voice, he said, "You sounded like your mother, lass."

Allandale spoke, and was relieved to hear a semblance of normality in his voice. "You're right, Catherine. I'm sure that ballad is Celtic in origin. My mother was forever telling me tales of the faeric folk—or people of the sidhe, as they're called in Ireland. She saw them once, she said, riding the crest of the hill near Ballylea. They beckoned to her, but she turned her horse and raced straight home!"

"Do you remember any of your mother's stories?" Aunt Louisa's voice was an odd mixture of tenderness and curiosity.

"I think so." He leaned back, stretching his feet in front of him, and stared into the flames. He spoke as though from a distance. "There was one that I particularly loved. It was about the faerie king, also." He looked at Catherine.

She was watching him, her face grave and quiet. "Go on."

"The Prince of Slievenamon, Lord Donal, had the most beautiful lady in the world for his wife. He loved the Lady Eithne very dearly; she was all the world to him." Allandale's tone was dreamlike. He looked from the fire to Catherine, then back into the flames. "One day Lady Eithne was asleep in the orchard and at the stroke of noon the king of the faeries appeared and stole her away."

"It was very foolish of her to fall asleep under an apple tree," Catherine's voice was serious. "Everyone knows the power of the faeries if you do that."

"Especially at noon," Allandale was equally grave.

"Of course. Then what happened?"

"Well, Lord Donal was distraught. He searched and searched for his wife. Finally, one day, he saw the shadowy horsemen riding the crest of the hill before him. With them was the Lady Eithne. Lord Donal spurred his horse and rode after them, but, just as he was about to reach them, they disappeared into the hillside."

"How terrible." Sophisticated Lady Lothian's face was full of the story's enchantment. Allandale smiled at her briefly, then went on.

"Lady Eithne's heart was broken, also. To see Lord Donal so close, yet be unable to go to him, was a torment she thought she could not bear. But the faerie king refused to release her from his enchantment.

"Finally, out of desperation, Lady Eithne made a proposal to her captor. Faeries, as you know, are terrified by fire. Eithne said to the faerie king, 'My Lord Donal loves me enough to ride to me through a sheet of flame.' The faerie king didn't believe her. Then Eithne said, 'If the Prince of Slievenamon braves the fire for my sake, will you release me and let me return to him?'"

Allandale paused and looked at the three rapt faces around him. He smiled sympathetically at the intensity of Catherine's face, then continued, his beautiful voice weaving a spell of its own. "The faerie king was no fool, as you can well imagine. 'Why should I grant you this trial?' he asked the lady. 'If my Lord Donal should fail,' she said, 'I will stay here and give you my service forever.' And so the king agreed."

The log in the fire crackled, showering sparks over the hearth. The sudden illumination flared, then quickly died down. The storyteller went on. "One day the Prince of Slievenamon was out riding on the hillside. His body and spirit were worn with longing for his wife. Death seemed to him sweeter than life without her. As he was thinking this, he saw the Lady Eithne in the distance. Quickly he spurred his horse, determined not to lose her this time. As he was almost upon the band of horsemen, she turned and stretched out her arms to him. Immediately, there appeared between them a sheet of flame."

The only sound in the room was Catherine's quickly indrawn breath.

"Remember now what Lord Donal had just been thinking. Death by fire, he thought, was preferable to life without his lady. So he spurred his horse right into the flame."

"Good man!" Even Sir Francis was caught up in the spell Allandale had woven.

Allandale smiled. "Well, he won his reward, sir. The crackling flames never harmed him, and when he reached the other side the horsemen of the sidhe were gone, fled back to the hollow hills. Only the Lady

Eithne was there, her arms still held out to him. And this time," Allandale concluded, "there was nothing to keep them apart."

The was complete silence for a moment, then Catherine heaved a sigh of satisfaction. "You're a born storyteller, James."

Aunt Louisa looked at Allandale in amazement. "He certainly is, my dear."

Allandale himself looked a little like a man surfacing from a dream. His voice sounded odd. "I'm surprised I remembered it as well as that. It was as though I had just heard it yesterday."

Catherine looked at him, her face full of the beautiful gravity he loved. She merely nodded, then rose and returned to the piano. Her nimble fingers struck the keys and the sounds of 'The Cherry Tree Carol' poured forth. Allandale followed her and joined his clear tenor to her soprano. Their voices melted together, soaring with the music. With a delighted smile, Catherine began another song and Sir Francis and Aunt Louisa joined in.

It was not long before father and aunt looked at each other. In perfect accord, they moved from the piano. "Well, it's been a long day," Sir Francis said. "I'm ready to call an end to it."

"I too will seek my bed," Aunt Louisa seconded him. Allandale came to her and, picking up her hand, gently kissed it. Catherine swallowed a lump in her throat at the glow on the old lady's face, and went to kiss her father.

And so, at ten o'clock at night, Allandale and Catherine were left alone. "Could they really have been that tired?" Catherine was mischievous.

"I think, rather, they were being tactful." Allandale watched as she returned to her chair. Her gown of dark green velvet set off the fine texture of her skin and bared the long, beautiful line of her throat. Her hair was worn in a heavy knot, seeming too heavy for the fragile neck that supported it. She looked at him gravely. He moved toward her. "I don't think I even have to tell you, do I?" he said.

She shook her head. "Nor I you."

He knelt before her and took her hands. "My heart," his voice was gentle, "I did you a very great wrong, and it does not seem just for me to profit by it. But I find I cannot regret the past, for it brought me you. I love you," he said, "I love you . . ."

Catherine looked at the man who had torn her from her home by violence. Because of him she had left the comfortable country of childhood and ventured into the wilderness of pain, fear, and love. "You are my life," she said to him. "You are my soul."

For a long moment the two remained silent, words too trivial for the depth of their communication. Then Catherine rose. "I will dismiss my maid," she said, "and wait for you."

There was a light in his eyes she had never seen before tonight, but he frowned slightly and held her gaze. "Are you sure, my love?"

The fire shone through his hair, almost making it seem to give off blue sparks. His light gray eyes seemed more startling than ever in their frame of long black lashes. Catherine looked at his mouth and caught her breath. "I'm sure," she said. And turned and went out the door.

The only feeling she was conscious of as she dismissed her maid and slowly dressed for bed was a feeling of joyous anticipation. This was the man she loved. Every flicker of expression on his face, every note in his voice, she felt in her heart. He had rarely touched her since their first violent encounter, but Catherine remembered only the joy of his few gentle caresses. The horror and fear of five months ago were gone. Or so she thought.

She picked up a brush and began to brush out her hair. It fell around her in a mantle of pale brown and gold, crackling and shining in the firelight. A knock sounded softly on the door and she called. "Come in."

Allandale paused on the threshold, his breath caught in his throat. Then he saw the welcoming glow on her face and moved forward swiftly. Her brush dropped forgotten to the floor and Catherine reached out to him. His arms around her, his face buried in the shining mass of her hair, his voice sounded strange to his own ears. "My love," was all he could say. "My little love."

Catherine raised her head from his shoulder and gently traced the line of his eyes, his nose, his mouth. "It almost frightens me, James," she said, "this thing between us. It has filled my world." She looked at him seriously. "I'm so afraid I'll lose you."

"Never fear, my love." A smile played irresistibly along his mouth. "You're stuck with me for life. And believe me, I plan to stick like a leech!"

She smiled back at him, but the darkness in her eyes failed to lift. "I hope so, my love. Oh my love, I hope so!" And raised the softness of her lips to his.

"Catherine," the word was almost a moan as his mouth came down on hers, shutting out the fire, the room, everything but him. Her body arched back to melt into his, slowly her mouth opened for him. For a magic moment, time stood still for Catherine and the flaming desire Allandale was trying to control began to beat in her as well. She was conscious of nothing save the feel of his hands and his lips. Then he swung her into his arms and laid her on the bed.

His kisses were harder and more demanding. His hands slid into her hair and suddenly time rolled back. The weight of an alien body pressing her down, a cruel mouth that thrust into hers and robbed her breath. She began to tremble. "Stop it!" a part of her mind cried. "This is James!" But, uncontrollably, the nightmare of suffocation and entrapment began to reenact itself. She struggled for air as all her senses screamed to escape. Still part of her fought for him, but the nightmare moved in and blotted out everything else.

It was a moment before Allandale realized what was

happening. His own desire beat so strongly that the change in Catherine was total before he realized it. Then he felt with horror her struggle to thrust him away from her, the uncontrollable shaking of her body. As he pulled back, he heard the painful whistle of her breath as she fought for air. He retreated from her as though he had been scalded, to the other side of the room by the windows, where he watched her struggle to control herself with anguish in his eyes.

Gradually the shaking stopped, and the dreadful hoarse breathing. Catherine sat for a moment, the long fall of her hair masking her face, then slowly, bitterly, she raised her head and looked at him. He was standing perfectly still, frozen, in front of the window. His own breathing was uneven, his face haggard with shock. "God help me," he said, "what have I done to you?"

She cried out, then, in denial. "It's not you, James. It's me. The nightmare again."

"I know. But because of what I did, I'm part of it."

The tears slowly streaked her young and anguished face. "I tried to stop it, James, but . . ."

"Don't!" His voice was like the crack of a whip. There was a pause as he tried to get hold of himself. "Don't blame yourself, my love. This is my doing." His voice shook with the emotion he was trying to control. "And to think I was congratulating myself on having found you that way."

She made a small movement of protest. "I will get over it, James, that stupid nightmare. We were born to love each other. I won't let it stand in our way."

Across the room the two pairs of gray eyes met. He didn't say the words that were in both their minds, "But you haven't gotten over it since you were nine years old." They stood on either side of a deep, dark chasm, helpless to move any closer. Catherine's words, "We were born to love each other," echoed in their ears.

Allandale said, "I wish to hell it was a sheet of fire. It would be easier."

XII

For to withstand her look I am not able,
Yet can I not hide me in no dark place . . .

—SIR THOMAS WYATT

As the slow hours of the night ticked by, Allandale stood by the windows of his room and looked out, seeing nothing. His mind was numb with horror. Catherine's face. That dreadful hoarse breathing. The mask that usually disguised James Pembrook's feelings was gone and what looked out from his eyes was naked pain and guilt. That he, who loved her, had done this to her. His own actions had forged the sword that lay between them.

As the initial shock began to wear off and his mind began to function, the full implication of what had happened struck him. His love for Catherine was not of the spirit only. The difficulty he had experienced living with her before would be magnified a thousandfold. His fingers cramped painfully on the sill as he thought of this. He desired her. He desired her as he had never desired anyone or anything. It was a flame within him, one that threatened to consume him.

The pale gray of his eyes had turned smoky. A sound was dragged unwillingly from his throat. *My God, my God*, he thought. *How can I do it?* "I'm so afraid I'll lose you," she had said.

As the dawn touched the sky, Allandale heard her call out from the room next door. His breathing stopped altogether as he listened. She was having a nightmare. The cords on his neck stood out and a muscle twitched in his cheek as he stood silent, helpless to go and comfort her. Gradually the sounds ceased, and he knew that she had wakened. He could feel her distress, her self-blame. And that too was an added burden for him to bear.

His face looked as though it was carved out of marble. This tragedy was entirely of his making. He would have to be the one to support it. *It will not destroy us,* he determined. I shall learn to make do with what I have. And God help us both, he thought.

As the weeks after Christmas moved along, it became apparent to both Sir Francis and Aunt Louisa that there was something very wrong between Allandale and Catherine. They seemed to be in a perfect harmony. No one seeing them together could have a moment's doubt as to the depth of their feeling for each other.

"But, Francis, there's something almost frightening in the air here." Aunt Louisa spoke perfectly seriously.

"I know," Sir Francis looked very worried. "It's difficult to put one's finger on just what is wrong, but something is obviously very wrong indeed."

"James looks exhausted," Aunt Louisa stated flatly. "He works like a madman all day, and obviously isn't sleeping at night."

"Cathy isn't much better. There's a look in her eyes, when she thinks no one is watching her, that haunts me. She looks . . ." Sir Francis searched for a word, "I don't like to be melodramatic, but she looks tragic."

"If ever two people were made for each other, it is James and Catherine."

"I know." Sir Francis ran a hand through his hair. "I'll try to talk to Cathy."

Aunt Louisa nodded agreement. "Something has got to be done."

With these thoughts in mind, Sir Francis approached his daughter. It was a cold, wet day and all the candles were lit in the drawing room. Catherine was at the piano, and the aching sadness of the music caused Sir Francis's clear blue eyes to darken. He stood for a moment at the door watching his daughter. Her face was quiet and grave, ineffably sad. As she lifted her eyes to his, the expression in them caused Sir Francis's nails to dig into his palms. He ached to gather her in his arms, but knew he couldn't.

Taking a deep breath to calm himself, he moved toward her. "Cathy," his voice was unutterably gentle, "do you want Lady Lothian and me to leave?"

She dropped her eyes to the piano and idly picked out a few notes. When she spoke, her voice was tight with rigidly controlled emotion. "It won't make any difference, Papa. It's probably better if you stay."

Sir Francis took the plunge. "My darling, you know how I love you. Can't I help you?"

Her voice was hopeless. "No one can help me, Papa."

"My God, Cathy," This voice cracked. "What is wrong? You look like a ghost. James looks like a man who has reached the end of his tether . . ."

"Don't!" She got her voice under control and went on. "Leave it, Papa. There's nothing you or James can do." Her small, elegant head, crowned with shining braids, was bowed over the piano. Then she raised her dark gray eyes and looked fully at her father.

Instinctively, he reached out to her, but she shook her head. "Cathy," he said urgently, "surely if you love each other. . . ."

She rubbed her temples as though she had a headache. "That's the problem," she said in a low voice. "Ironically, if we loved each other less . . . if James loved me less, it might be all right." Her voice took on a note of desperation. "But it's not all right, Papa. It's terrible. And it will only get worse. How can I do this to him? Every time he looks at me . . ." her voice broke. "What can I do?" she whispered, "what can I do?"

Her father caught her in a warm embrace, and felt her stiff, unyielding to the comfort he was trying to give. Dimly he began to perceive what was wrong. "Darling, can't you . . ." he began, only to be interrupted by Catherine's pulling away from him. By the way she held her head and the listening look on her face, he knew she had heard something.

"It's James," she said. "He's been out riding." They both looked out the window at the cold, unceasing fall of rain. "He rides for hours every day. Even in this," she gestured toward the rain. "God help me," she said in unconscious echo, "what have I done to him?"

It was several moments before Allandale's step sounded in the hall. How she had heard him before, Sir Francis didn't know. The steps hesitated for a moment at the door of the drawing room, then the door opened and he came in. The rain and the cold had brought color into his face, and rain still dripped from his lashes. Spots of wet stained his clothes where his rain cloak had failed to protect him. He had the look of a man who was living solely on his nerves. He glanced at Sir Francis, then went straight to Catherine. She smiled at him. "You look like a sealchie from the Western Isles," she said.

His eyes had lit the moment they rested on her. Now he too smiled. "A sealchie?" he inquired.

"They are mythical creatures—great seals in the water who take the shape of a man on earth. You look," she teased, "like you've just surfaced."

"And I'm probably dripping all over the carpet. I know," he said. "I just thought I'd look in on you. I'd better go change." He turned to go.

"James!" Catherine called. He turned back, surprised. "This came for you in the mail." She rose and slowly crossed to him, holding out a letter. He looked at it, then back to her sharply. "It's from Davy Aberfan," she said. "You'd better take it with you and read it." For a moment he remained still, looking at her, then nodded, turned, and left the room.

Catherine stood still at the door. Finally, she turned and met her father's compassionate eyes. "I've just given him his way out," she said.

Allandale stood by the fire in his room, the unopened letter in his hands. Finally, with a sudden movement of determination, he opened it.

"James," Davy wrote. "Canning is very anxious to talk to you. There are plans afoot for a congress of the Great Powers to discuss withdrawing the army occupation. He is nervous. It's imperative you come—he is ripe for persuasion. —Davy."

Allandale transferred his gaze from the letter to the flames. Now, when he wanted to throw the weight of his influence into the fray, he couldn't. He had promised himself not to leave Catherine. His mouth set in hard lines, and he began to undress. He had stripped to his shirt and breeches and was about to ring for his valet to help him with his boots when a knock sounded on the door. He knew, instantly, who it was.

The door opened and Catherine entered. She closed the door behind her and remained before it, on the far side of the room. She went right to the point. "What did Davy want?"

"He wants me to meet with Canning."

"Are you going?"

"No."

"I see." She drew a deep breath. "Why not?"

He looked at her a moment in silence. Then, "You know why not."

"Yes." Another breath. "I want you to go, James."

He shook his head.

"Yes," she said.

"If I go, Catherine, it will be because I have committed myself to try to change what I feel is a disastrous policy for England, for Europe. I cannot do this successfully if I am—distracted." He rubbed his hand tiredly across his face. "You couldn't come with me," he said wearily.

"I know," she said.

Across the length of the room their eyes met. He made an abrupt gesture, and turned to face the fire.

"I need time, James," she said gently. "Come back for the baby." He didn't turn from the fire. "I'll tell Papa and Aunt Louisa you're leaving tomorrow."

She was gone. She had released him from the intolerable situation they were in. He could still feel her presence in his room. . . . He closed his eyes in pain. She was right. He had to go.

Davy was talking. He had been talking ever since Allandale had arrived in London yesterday. "Canning can't stand Castlereagh, of course, but it's more than just personal disliking. He doesn't trust this policy . . ."

"Davy—enough. In five minutes' time I can find out for myself just what Canning thinks." They were at the door of Canning's house and in the promised five minutes had had their outer garments taken and been ushered into Canning's study. He rose as they entered, holding out his hand to Allandale. "I am so glad you could come, Lord Allandale. Aberfan, good of you."

Canning reseated himself behind his desk and looked at Allandale sharply. "Well. You were in Spain for the whole show, Lord Allandale. You were in Vienna. You were at Waterloo. If anyone has a right to say something about our postwar policy, it's you." he paused. "Aberfan tells me you have a good deal to say. "Well?" He looked challengingly at Allandale.

Allandale was precise. "We fought a bloody war in Europe, Mr. Canning. We fought it to protect Europe because if Europe falls to tyranny we are naturally endangered, also. However," his voice was clipped, "it seems to me we are in danger of winning the war but losing the peace."

Canning raised his eyebrows. "How?"

"What are Castlereagh's objectives? First of all, he wants to maintain a balance of power in Europe. That is why he agreed to carving up Poland and Germany and Italy—each of the victors got some of the spoils. No one got it all. So he thinks they are satisfied. The guiding force of his present foreign policy is to guard against any further French aggression. This is nonsense."

Canning leaned forward. "You don't see France as a threat, then?"

"Certainly not at the moment. Napoleon is very safely locked up on Saint Helena. Even if he managed to escape, I doubt if he could gather an army of any size at all. France is sick of war."

Canning nodded. "Yes, you argued very well for that point when you persuaded the cabinet to cut down the army of occupation. In fact," Canning looked at his hands, "you were so persuasive that we are initiating a congress to discuss withdrawing the entire army."

"So I understand."

Canning looked directly at Allandale. "You disapprove, my lord?"

"Not at all."

"Then what, in your opinion, is the danger in our present policy?"

Allandale smiled and, almost against his will, Canning found himself smiling back. "The danger, as well you know, Mr. Canning, is the so-called Holy Alliance, and Lord Castlereagh's unhappy yearning to use it as a forum for consulting on all European matters."

"The Holy Alliance," Canning mused, "brainchild of Czar Alexander and signed on September twenty-sixth by Russia, Prussia, and Austria. A personal union of sovereigns, pledging themselves to act on Christian principles."

Allandale's tone was dry. "The major Christian principle of those three nations is the perpetuation and enlargement of their own already vast powers and territories."

Canning was rueful. "I am afraid you are correct, Lord Allandale. But what is our alternative? As you pointed out, Lord Castlereagh's major policy is the maintenance of the balance of power in Europe. England doesn't want any European territory. All we want is markets for our merchandise. We want peace, Lord Allandale."

Allandale's mouth was grim. "If you keep giving in to the autocracies, letting them gobble up nation after nation, you aren't going to have peace, Mr. Canning. You are going to have a war to end all wars. And we, inevitably, will be involved." As Canning's eyes leaped to his, he raised a hand. "I don't say it will happen in our lifetime. But it will happen. The desire of the smaller nations for self-government cannot be ignored with impunity, Mr. Canning. England's role should not be to aid and abet in their oppression. But this," with effort he kept his voice dispassionate, "this is precisely what we will be doing if we allow ourselves to act in concert with the nations of the Holy Alliance."

Canning's tone was dry. "This kind of argument will hold little weight with Lord Castlereagh. He is far from being sympathetic to the aspiring nationalism of the smaller countries."

Allandale's voice was silky. "True, but I do not think he would be insensible to the political ramifications of this issue. If we participate in a series of meetings with the Eastern autocracies, we might involve England in common action with them against the nationalistic rebellions of their present subjects. These rebellions might, in the eyes of the people of England, be eminently legitimate. If such was the case, the English people might well signify their disapproval of the government's actions by, ah, voting it out of power?"

Canning's lips were taut. "So they might, Lord Allandale. So you think Castlereagh's dream of sitting down at future congresses with the other Great Powers is dangerous?"

"Dangerous and stupid." Allandale's finely cut nostrils dilated in contempt. "It is, in fact, the most half-assed idea I've ever heard of. It is in the sixth article of the treaty. What does it mean? Who is to represent the

Powers at these meetings? Princes? Ministers? Is it a permanent organization, with a set timetable for meetings? Who is to prepare the agenda? What are the rules of procedure? Is anyone assigned the duty of collecting data for the objective study of any question? No, Mr. Canning," he said, "it is a stupidly conceived and shoddily planned proposal. And yes, it is dangerous."

Canning frowned. "So you do disapprove of this upcoming congress?"

"No. You have to meet once, to discuss the question of the army of occupation. But that should be it."

Canning made up his mind. "We need to send someone to Vienna to make arrangements for the congress. Someone who can find out some behind-the-scenes information for us. Will you go? I'm sure Lord Castlereagh would be delighted to have you. Wellington gave you quite a recommendation."

Allandale hesitated. "I must be in England during March."

Canning shrugged. "If there's more to do, you can always go back."

Allandale rose and held out his hand. "I'll go."

As they ate dinner together later that evening, Davy said curiously, "Did you mean what you said, James, about a war?"

Allandale's face was perfectly sober. "I do, Davy. Canning is no revolutionary, so I didn't push it. But if the national desires of the smaller nations are not realized, the whole of Europe will explode in our faces one day. Napoleon," he said, "will be as nothing compared to the holocaust that would be unloosed then."

XIII

How like a winter bath my absence been
From thee, the pleasure of the fleeting year!
What freezings have I felt, what dark days seen!

—WILLIAM SHAKESPEARE

Catherine reread and folded Allandale's last letter and locked it in a small chest on the table beside her bed. In the last two months her figure had become much bulkier. Neither her height nor her clothing could conceal her pregnancy any longer. And with advancing pregnancy had come a merciful cocoon of numbness. She walked about the house, oblivious to all but the most pressing demands on her attention. The movement of the baby within her, a letter from Allandale, these were her world.

Sir Francis had decided to remain with Catherine until the baby was born. He looked at his daughter's alabaster face and her bulky silhouette with concern. "I'm worried about Cathy," he confided to Aunt Louisa, who had remained at Barton Abbey also. "She drifts around like a shadow. Half the time she doesn't hear what one is saying to her."

"I know what you mean," Aunt Louisa said. "But perhaps it's best. Grief, that bleak look she had right after he left, surely that was worse?"

He had to agree. "But all the same, I'm going to get a doctor from London down here. If anything should be wrong . . ."

"I'm sure nothing is wrong. Catherine is a healthy

young girl. But if it will make you feel better, by all means get someone from London."

He nodded decisively. "I will. I think I'll go up this afternoon. I'd better tell Cathy." Aunt Louisa watched him go out, an understanding smile on her face. It will make him feel better to be doing something, she thought. Men always feel so helpless at times like this.

Catherine, listening to her father, had come to the same conclusion. "I'm perfectly all right, Papa, but if it will make you happy, I will see this doctor. In fact," she said, improvising rapidly, "I'm sure you'll find it difficult to get a doctor down here right away. Why not stay in London a few days, and come back down with him?"

Sir Francis brightened perceptibly. "That's a good idea, Cathy. I want to talk to Addington about this new tariff. So criminally stupid."

She smiled warmly at him. "Poor darling, I'm afraid I haven't been much company for you."

"Not at all," he hastened to reassure her. "I'm only going because of the doctor."

"I know, Papa, I know."

He looked at her worriedly, and she reached up to kiss him on the cheek. "I'm fine, really, Papa. When you're in London, perhaps you'll hear some news of James."

"I'll certainly inquire."

"Splendid," she said warmly. "When are you leaving?"

"I may as well go after lunch."

"Fine." She tucked her arm in his. "I'll tell Challoncer to have John get the barouche ready for you. I'm afraid James took the phaeton." As they walked to the door, a footman entered, letter in hand.

"For you, my lady."

Catherine recognized the small, precise writing, and her pale face lit with happiness. "I'll go and put some things together, Cathy," Sir Francis said, and tactfully left her alone. Slowly she broke the seal and opened the letter. His previous letters had been full of the details of his embassy. She knew exactly whom he had seen and what had been said. The Congress was set for September at Aix-la-Chapelle. Czar Alexander was firmly under Metternich's thumb, and Catherine knew that Allandale expected some kind of maneuver at the congress to try to draw England into the orbit of the Holy Alliance. This letter was different, brief and personal.

"My heart, I leave Vienna tomorrow for England. I shall be with you soon. My thoughts have never left you. But, of course, you know that. —James."

The child gave a strong kick, and Catherine laughed, her hands over her stomach. "He's coming!" she cried. "He's coming!" It wasn't until the flood or relief engulfed her that she realized what she had feared most. That he couldn't bring himself to come again. With surprising lightness, she moved to the door. "Aunt Louisa!" she called. "He's coming!"

When Allandale reached London, he immediately called on Canning. "Your reports were of enormous interest," Canning told him. "How did you manage to find out so much in so little time?"

Allandale smiled. "Vienna is full of gossips. I simply listened. I'm glad it was useful."

"Have you seen Castlereagh yet?"

"No. I came to see you first." He paused, and Canning studied the sculptured face before him, the remarkable pale eyes dark now with fatigue.

"How old are you my lord?" Canning asked suddenly.

Someone else had once surprised him with that question. He shook his head as though to clear it and answered automatically, "Twenty-six." Then he paused, an arrested look in his eyes. "No, twenty-seven," he corrected himself. "As of last week."

Canning looked deeply surprised. "Twenty-seven— somehow one forgets how young you are."

Allandale rubbed his forehead, his movements slow.

He looked as though he was very tired, not merely travel-tired, but with a deep weariness that went beyond the body.

"I don't feel very young," he said. "There is one more thing you should know. Alexander is planning to propose a general league of the Great Powers—England included, of course—which would guarantee to each monarch his throne *and* his present territory."

Canning whistled in surprise.

"Precisely. Even Castlereagh won't buy that. So make what gains you can."

"When are you going to see him?"

"Tomorrow morning. I'll break the news to him and leave you to press home with it."

"Where can I reach you, Allandale?"

"In Somerset. I am going to Barton Abbey to see my wife."

Canning was left to wonder at the distressed look that had briefly flickered across Allandale's face as he said that. Then he remembered that Lady Allandale was shortly expecting a child. He must be worried about her, he thought.

Allandale hardly noticed the bright, sunny countryside of his native land. He drove his matched grays at a spanking pace, a small part of his conscious mind noticing the road and the incidentals of travel. The rest of his mind was occupied with one thought: *I'll see her again.* He had been busy with work he felt worth doing, but always he was aware of the emptiness inside left by Catherine's absence. It was a wound that never ceased to ache, no matter where he was or what he was doing. He was worn out from it.

As the upper windows of Barton Abbey came into view, he felt his breath rasp in his throat. Surely, he thought, surely this time he could manage it. To see her, talk to her, surely that would be enough. . . .

He pulled into the stable yard. It was one of those March days that betray one into thinking that winter

had gone for good. Small green shoots pushed hopefully up through the wet earth and pale green covered
the fields. The barrenness of winter was slowly being
obliterated.

Catherine was in the garden looking hopefully at the
early signs of spring. She had lifted her face to the
warmth of the sun, stretching like a flower toward the
sky, when she heard his step. She turned, and suddenly
a memory flashed into her mind: the memory of another garden and a young girl fearfully awaiting her
unknown husband. But this was not a stranger. This
was the man she loved most in the world. With hands
outstretched, she went to meet him.

He stood stock still as she moved awkwardly toward
him. His face was ashen. His eyes, appalled, met hers.
"Catherine!" He was white to the lips.

She stopped before him and looked at him steadily.
Her instinct told her his distress was due to more than
just her altered appearance.

Allandale felt himself awash with panic. Stupid, he
told himself, you knew she was pregnant. But, as he
looked and looked at her face, pure as crystal, he knew
he hadn't let himself really believe it. He had been
afraid to believe it. God, he had to say something to
her. . . .

But Catherine spoke first. As always, she went
straight to the heart of his feelings. "Don't look like
that, James. I have no intention of dying in childbirth."

The spoken words released the terror that was chok-
ing him. He pulled her roughly into his arms and held
her tightly, his cheek against her hair. "You had better
not," he said, his voice harsh. "If I lost you . . ."

Her voice was muffled by his shoulder. "I am perfectly fine. You aren't going to get rid of me so easily,
I promise you."

He released her slowly and held her away from him,
his eyes searching hers. "Are you sure, my heart?"

"I am sure." Her eyes were full of understanding.
"You are not going to lose me, so stop being such a

figure of tragedy." Her gaze was suddenly severe. "You make me nervous."

Her tone had its intended effect. He managed a laugh. "Oh, God, Catherine. I'm sorry. I've been making a first-class ass out of myself."

She reached up and covered his hands as they lay on her shoulder. "You have, rather."

His laugh this time was more genuine. "You'd never know it, the way I've been carrying on, but I've actually delivered a baby."

Catherine looked at him in awe. "You did? When?"

"In Spain." He reached out a gentle hand to caress her cheek. "I was the only one around at the time. I must say I did little more than follow Maria's orders." He frowned. "But she was a big peasant woman and this was her third child. Whereas you. . . ." He looked from her finely molded face to her delicate wrists.

"You are not to worry," she said contentedly. "I don't plan to have any trouble at all. I've given the baby strict orders."

He looked at her confident face and felt some of the burden ease from him. He was with her again. He smiled at her, a happy, unshadowed smile that lit his eyes from within. "Don't I rate a welcome-home kiss?"

Gravely she looked back at him. He looked very tired, but he looked at peace. Her beautiful smile warmed him and she raised her face to his. His kiss was gentle, sweet, and loving: a blessing and a promise. Catherine nestled her head on his shoulder. "Oh, I have longed for you, James."

His arm cradled her. His hand gently caressed her hair. "I know, my heart," he said. "I know."

Later, as they made their way back to the house, they met Aunt Louisa in the hall arranging a vase of greens. "James!" Her face brightened and Allandale bent to kiss her cheek.

"Aunt Louisa. I'm delighted to see you. Catherine, my love," he turned to her, "don't you think you ought to lie down before dinner? I would like a word with Aunt Louisa."

Catherine smiled mischievously. "She'll only tell you the same thing I did, James. Why don't you talk to Papa, too? He dragged a doctor all the way down from London." She grasped the stair railing. "See you at dinner. Reassure him please, Aunt." And slowly she began to mount the stairs.

Aunt Louisa led the way into the small saloon. She seated herself and smiled at him. "Really, James, Catherine is right. She is doing very well. Sir Francis had Sir Lawrence Melton down from London to see her, and he confirmed what Dr. Kiley had said all along. Catherine is perfectly well and there is no reason to expect any trouble with the confinement."

His pale eyes had a strained look to them. "Are you sure, Aunt Louisa?"

"Perfectly sure, my dear boy." She hesitated, then went on. "I know what you are afraid of. Catherine's case is not at all like your mother's. Your mother's heart wasn't strong, James. She had had rheumatic fever as a child, you know, and a long, difficult labor was dangerous for her because of that. Catherine's health is excellent. She is young and strong and, from the looks of her, the child isn't going to be overly big."

Some of the strain in his eyes lifted as he listened to her. He reached out and covered her hand with his. "Thank you, Aunt Louisa. And thank you for taking care of Catherine." His smile was warm. "I lost my mother, but over the years I was fortunate enough to find another."

Aunt Louisa listened to his retreating footsteps with unshed tears bright in her eyes. "Please God," she whispered, "let all go well."

XIV

Sing lullaby, as women do,
Wherewith they bring their babes to rest,
And lullaby can I sing too,
As womanly as can the best.

—GEORGE GASCOIGNE

For the weeks immediately preceding the birth of their child, Catherine and Allandale were happy. Her pregnancy had, for the time being, wiped away the gulf that separated them. Catherine's face gained color. The tiredness engraved on Allandale's bones disappeared. For a space of time they had only quiet joy in each other.

Catherine's activities were necessarily limited. But the weather stayed sunny and warm and she and Allandale spent their afternoons in the garden.

"I got a letter from Spain this morning," he told her one day.

"Oh?"

"There will be trouble soon, I'm afraid."

"Of course there will be," she returned. "No one of any character could stomach Ferdinand for long." They were sitting on a little bench near the rose garden. She reached over and put her hand on his, where it lay clenched on his knee. "I know," she said low, "it makes me angry, too."

There was a pause while both pursued their thoughts. Catherine bit her lips. "Will Ferdinand ask Russia for help if there is an uprising?"

She could feel his tenseness under her hand. "Assuredly he will. He will ask all his fellow monarchs to help him put down a rebellion of his disloyal subjects."

"England won't be a party to such an action!" Catherine was indignant. "Why we fought *for* Spain against Ferdinand just a few years ago. We can't turn around now and do the opposite."

"No," Allandale's voice was grim. "I doubt if we'd go that far. We may just not do anything, and let the Christian monarchs of the Holy Alliance go their own way."

Catherine sat silent for a moment, her brow thoughtful. Allandale looked at her curiously. "What are you thinking, my love?"

A sparkle of mischief came into her face. "There's only one thing to be done, James, so far as I can see."

"And what is that?"

"You must simply do your humble best to foster distrust and ill feeling among the members of the Holy Alliance."

An answering spark of mischief dawned in his eyes. "Do you know, I had had that very idea?"

"I thought you might have," she said demurely.

"I make a very odd Goddess of Discord, though."

"Not at all," Catherine told him. "I can just see you now, dribbling poisonous little nothings in the ear of Czar Alexander."

" 'Divide and conquer,' " Allandale chanted, and Catherine broke into the "Marseillaise." The sun smiled down on their young, laughing faces and strongly clasped hands.

Sir Francis and Aunt Louisa shared in their happiness. The glow that surrounded Catherine and Allandale spread its warmth, and the older couple basked in its reflection. They stood one morning in the French doors that led out to the garden.

"This is a marriage created out of fear," Sir Francis said. "When I saw my daughter go off with this man, it seemed to me I had made a mistake that would haunt me all my life. And now," he turned to Aunt Louisa, "it is only a cause of joy for me."

Aunt Louisa's formidable features softened. "She is a lovely girl, your Catherine, and she deserves the best." She looked at him directly, almost challengingly. "And in James that is just what she has gotten."

Sir Francis laughed at her. "Louisa, you don't have to ruffle your feathers at me. I know that. There is a power and a strength in that boy—I doubt if he even realizes what he is capable of."

Aunt Louisa sighed. "Catherine is his salvation, Francis. Because he loves her, he has a tie to the world." Her voice became fervent. "I pray to God that whatever went wrong between them before doesn't happen again."

Sir Francis's mouth set in lines of pain. "I hope so too, Louisa, I hope so too."

As they came into the house, the sound of the piano greeted them. Aunt Louisa raised her eyebrows at Sir Francis. It had been some time since Catherine had been able to reach the keyboard.

They entered the drawing room to see her standing sideways, picking out a melody with one hand. In the other, she held a sheet of music.

"I was up on the third floor," she said, "looking at the room we're going to use as a nursery, and I found some old music. It must have belonged to James's mother. It seems to be Irish."

Allandale himself walked in. "What's all this?" he asked.

"Oh, James," Catherine went to him. "Look what I found."

"It seems to quite a cache," he said.

Catherine picked out another tune on the piano, and lifted her voice with the music. "Do you know it?" she asked Allandale when she had finished.

He looked very sober. "It is about the English devastation of Ireland at the end of the seventeenth cen-

tury." But that old atrocity was far from his mind. The
words of the song ran around his brain. "Our day is
o'er," and "Shaun O'Dwyer of the Valley/Your
pleasure is no more." He looked at Catherine, her head
bent over another sheet of music, and his lips
tightened. He turned and his eyes met Sir Francis's.
With a sharp gesture, he put down the music and left
the room.

As the door closed behind him, Catherine looked
with surprise at her father. "He's worried about you,
Cathy," he said.

She looked grave. "I know he is. This baby had better make an appearance soon."

They had not long to wait. Two days later, Catherine was awakened by a pain in her back. She thought
little of it, but as the morning went on, the ache in her
back increased. She was standing at the bookshelves in
the library when a sudden sharp pain caused her to
gasp aloud. Allandale, whose nerves were attuned to
every nuance of expression on her face, jumped as
though he had been shot at. In a second he was by her
side, his face anxious. She smiled at him reassuringly.
"Don't look so worried, James. Truly, it will be all
right." She took a step and another pain shot through
her. "I think perhaps this baby is finally going to be
born," she said.

As the afternoon went by, Allandale became more
and more worried. The doctor had arrived and was
with Catherine. Aunt Louisa made periodic visits to the
library to assure Allandale and Sir Francis that all was
going well, and first babies took a long time. Neither
man could eat any dinner, and as the evening ticked
along, Allandale was becoming frantic. There was no
sound at all from upstairs.

Aunt Louisa arrived in the library at about eleven
o'clock. She had a frown on her face which she
smoothed away as she confronted the urgent look of
Allandale and Sir Francis. "She is being very brave,"

Aunt Louisa said. "Dr. Kiley says all is going normally. But it is slow." And for what seemed to Allandale the thousandth time, she said, "Don't worry."

At one o'clock in the morning, Allandale looked at Sir Francis and said, "I'm going up there." The older man met his eyes and nodded.

Catherine felt that she was living in a nightmare of pain. At first it had not been bad; the pains came only every few minutes and didn't last very long. But as the afternoon and evening progressed, it seemed to her that her body was being ripped and torn apart, with only seconds of respite between each bout of agony. As if from a great distance, she heard the voices of Dr. Kiley and Aunt Louisa. All her efforts were bent on bearing the pain without crying out. Mustn't scream, she thought, mustn't frighten James. And her nails tore into her palms and her teeth clenched together as the pain swept over her once more.

Allandale entered the room quietly. His already pale face turned paper-white as he saw Catherine on the bed, her body arched in agony. Dr. Kiley looked startled at his appearance, but Allandale went swiftly to him. "Why is it taking so long?"

Dr. Kiley heard the tense anguish in Allandale's voice and heaved a sigh. "Lady Allandale is very slender through the hips and the baby is big."

Allandale's eyes went black with fear. "Oh my God."

"No need to look like that," the doctor spoke gruffly. "There's no reason to think there is any danger. She is having a hard time, though." His voice softened perceptibly. "She is putting up a good fight, my lord. But it is going to be a while yet."

Allandale heard Catherine's sharply indrawn breath and winced in pain. He looked at the doctor. "If she is fighting the pain, holding back, instead of pushing with it, she is making things slower, isn't she?"

Dr. Kiley looked astonished. "Yes, my lord. "We've tried to get her to cry out, but she won't." With steady purpose, Allandale turned and went over to Catherine. Fear and helpless anger swept over him as he looked at her. Her long hair had escaped its confining ribbons and was tangled and matted with sweat. Her lips were swollen from her teeth tearing at them, her face a mask of agony.

Through the hell of pain Catherine heard his voice. She opened her eyes and gazed desperately into his. "Listen to me, my love," his voice was strong and calm. "I am going to help you." He reached for her hands and her fingers clutched at his. As the pain swept over her again, she could hear him saying, "Don't fight it, Catherine. Give in. Go with it. Yell, Catherine. Yell." She clung desperately to his hands and concentrated the tiny part of her consciousness that was not consumed by pain on his voice. She cried out.

As the pain receded momentarily, Allandale smiled at her warmly. "Good, my love." She managed a shaky smile in return before the pain began again. . . .

At ten after three on the morning of March 18, Catherine's child was born. They had sent Allandale out of the room five minutes before, and he stood tensely in the hallway, listening. He heard Catherine give a loud cry, then there was the sound of a baby crying. He leaned against the wall and raised a shaking hand to his face.

Twenty minutes later, Aunt Louisa came out. "You can come back now, James," she said softly. He entered the room tentatively and stopped on the threshold, his eyes flying toward the bed Catherine was lying propped up. Her hair had been braided and lay over her shoulder. The skin under her eyes looked bruised, and she looked deathly tired. But in the crook of her arm was a tiny bundle, and her smile was lovely.

Her eyes met his, a trace of anxiety in them. "Come and meet your daughter, James," she said. He walked slowly to the bed and gazed down at the baby nestled in her arm. Its face was tiny, its silky skin was red, but otherwise it was a miniature of his own face that he saw. He looked from his daughter to his wife. His voice unsteady, "My two girls," he said.

Radiance washed across Catherine's tired face. "I never thought a girl would give me that much trouble," she said. Her hand reached out for his. "My love . . ." Aunt Louisa left the room to tell Sir Francis.

The sun was turning the sky pink when Allandale said good-bye to the doctor at the front door of Barton Abbey. "You're the best midwife I've ever worked with, my lord," Dr. Kiley teased. "If you plan to go into business, let me know."

"Absolutely not." Allandale shook his head in horror. "My nerves couldn't stand it." The doctor laughed and shook his head.

"That's a very brave lass you've got, my lord. In two months' time she should be right as rain. Then you can see about a son."

Allandale closed the door and slowly traced his steps upstairs. He stopped for a moment outside Catherine's room, but all was silent. The baby had been put to sleep in her dressing room and she too was asleep. He entered his own room but stood for a long while without undressing. There was the sound of activity in the house before Allandale finally lay down to try to get a few hours' rest.

When next he saw Catherine, all traces of the night's vigil had been swept from his face. The afternoon sun poured into her room, lighting the gold threads in her hair. Allandale looked at her, sitting up in bed, her hair tied back with a ribbon, looking absurdly youthful, and he shook his head ruefully. "You hardly look old enough to be playing with dolls," he told her.

"Nonsense, my lord. I'll have you know that in exactly one week's time I shall be eighteen years old."

"Christ." He rose from his seat beside her bed and paced to the window. He stood with his back to her.

"Catherine, you make me feel thoroughly ashamed of myself."

"Don't be silly," her voice was impatient. "You're not exactly decrepit yourself. James, I want to talk to you about something important."

He turned toward her, the remnant of a frown still on his face. "And what, besides your embarrassing youth, is so important?"

"The baby's name."

"Oh." He came back toward the bed. "Well, my love, what would you like to call her? Not Catherine," he said. "There can be only one Catherine."

She smiled and reached out to take his hand. "No, not Catherine," she agreed. "Besides, she doesn't look like me at all. She's the image of you. I should like," she said softly, "to call her Eileen."

For a moment he was silent, gazing down at their clasped hands. Then he bent and kissed the top of her head. "Thank you, my heart. I should like that very much."

She smiled up at him mistily. "There's only one more question of importance we have to settle."

"What is that?"

"Surely you got my hint. Whatever are you going to get me, James, for my birthday?"

His face lit up with mischief, momentarily making him look absurdly youthful himself. "As for that, my love, you will simply have to wait and see."

XV

Catherine came downstairs for the first time on her birthday. In spite of her protestations, Allandale insisted on carrying her down the stairs. Aunt Louisa and Sir Francis welcomed her into the drawing room by chorusing "Happy Birthday." Catherine kissed them both, her face reflecting her pleasure. In her ears shone diamond earrings, a gift from her father.

"I'm tired of being treated like an invalid," she told them all. "It feels wonderful just to see downstairs again!"

"I understand the cook has outdone himself in your honor, my dear child," Aunt Louisa said. "And, not to be outdone by the servants, I have a remembrance for your birthday myself."

Catherine took the proffered box with a smile of thanks, which turned to awe as she saw what was in it. Suspended from a slender golden chain was a pendant—the most beautiful emerald Catherine had ever seen. "Oh, Aunt Louisa," she breathed, and looked at the old woman, a question in her eyes.

"Lord Lothian gave that to me for a wedding present," she said. "It would have gone to my daughter. I want you to have it, dear child."

"You honor me, Aunt Louisa," Catherine said seriously. Then her smile, as warm as an embrace, broke through. "Thank you!"

Sir Francis broke the momentary silence. "Well, this is a day for family treasures, it seems. Your grandfather wrote me a while ago to tell me to inform you that he is going to send you your grandmother's engagement ring."

Catherine felt tears rise to her eyes. "Oh, Papa."

"I know, darling," he said. "He was saving it for your wedding, you know. I told you he'd come around, eventually. He loves you too much to be estranged from you. Besides," his eyes glinted, "I rather think he likes having a war hero for a grandson."

"What?" Allandale's head swung around.

Sir Francis looked innocent. "I merely mentioned a few of the more well-known facts of your career, James."

Aunt Louisa put in, "So that was what got Alexander started asking me all those questions about James."

Allandale looked at the three mirthful faces watching him. "I have a feeling I'm not going to like this," he said.

"Don't worry, James," Sir Francis said. "Lord Carberry admires only two things in a man—Scottish blood and bravery. You didn't have the first, so we had to rely rather heavily on the second."

"How did you establish *your* credentials, sir?" Allandale was plainly not happy with this turn of events.

"Oh, I merely told him that I didn't give a damn what he said or did, I was going to marry his daughter anyway. That speech effectively established my bravery. No one ever talks like that to Lord Carberry."

An unwilling smile tugged at the corners of Allandale's long mouth. "I think I would have preferred that route myself."

"Well, you didn't get the chance, James," Catherine said. "I know you hate it, but you're just going to have to learn to accept your reputation gracefully. You can practice looking heroic in your mirror." Over the general laughter, she continued, looking expectant, "Well, James?"

He caught his breath. "Well, what?"

She looked hurt. "Everyone else has given me a birthday present."

Sir Francis grinned. "For as long as I can remember, Cathy has behaved as though her birthday were on a level with the signing of the Magna Charta or some other great national event."

"And of course you never encouraged her, sir." Allandale turned to his wife. "You'll have to come with me, my love."

A sparkle came to Catherine's eyes. "Certainly," she said, suppressed excitement written all over her face.

Allandale took her arm and guided her to the front of the house, slowly down the steps and toward the stable. "Stay here," he told her, and moved off swiftly. A few minutes later he returned, leading a silver-gray colt on a halter. Speechless, Catherine took in the face, its wedge shape showing his Arab blood, down the sloping line of shoulder, smooth back, and long, straight legs. She moved closer and the colt turned to look at her, small ears flicked forward. Her eyes flew to Allandale.

"He's a year old, and never been ridden. Happy birthday, my love." The look of a small boy who successfully pulls off a big surprise was on his face. Catherine looked from him to the colt and back again. She swallowed hard, then smiled at him with equal delight.

"Thank you, James," her voice was throaty with emotion. Slowly she approached the horse from the front, her hand held out before her. He pulled his head, up, then let her stroke his velvet muzzle, even going so far as to rub his head against her.

Allandale watched as she made friends with the colt. She was a superb rider, he knew. Now, watching her stroke and whisper to the nervous colt, calming and gentling him, he knew he had chosen well. The look in Catherine's eyes as she came toward him while the groom led the colt away caused him to break once again into a boyish grin. She laughed up at him. "I knew it had to be something special from the way you've been acting, but I never dreamed. . . . Oh, James," she heaved a sigh and slipped her arm through his, "he's beautiful."

"I'm glad you like him, my love." They walked slowly toward the house. "I have a cousin in Ireland who raises and sells horses. I wrote to him several months ago, and this colt is the result. He's been in Wales at Davy's since February."

"I didn't know you kept in touch with any of your Irish relations, James."

"Well, there aren't many of them. My grandparents are dead and my mother's only brother died while I was in Spain. The property belongs to Michael O'Leary, the cousin who raises horses. Oddly enough, I met him in the Peninsula. He had just received the news of my uncle's death and was selling out to return home. He got a few horses for me when I returned to England, and they were magnificent. So when I wanted a colt for you, I wrote to him."

"Did he find you Sultan?"

"Yes." He grinned. "I know you always envied me him, so I thought I'd get you an Arab of your own."

"Well," she said, "this has been the best birthday I can remember.

She echoed that sentiment later in the evening when they were all sitting around the fire in the drawing room. Catherine's face was showing signs of fatigue, but nothing could quench the happiness in her eyes. "Even Eileen gave me a present," she said. "She actually smiled at me when I was holding her before."

"Probably gas," Sir Francis said.

"It was not!" She was indignant. "She recognized me. I'm sure of it!"

"Of course she did," Allandale soothed her. "Who else goes hysterical with delight every time she sneezes?"

"You do," she accused him.

He grinned. "Well, I must admit she is a remarkably beautiful baby."

"She's the image of you," Catherine protested.

"I know." He lowered his eyes modestly. Everyone laughed, and Allandale rose and went over to Catherine. "Come on, my love. Eileen is tucked away in her bed, and you should be in yours."

Catherine rose and felt her knees give way a bit. "I *am* tired," she confessed. "Goodnight Papa, Aunt Louisa. I'll see you in the morning."

As Allandale lifted her in his arms to carry her upstairs, she slipped her arms around his neck and put her cheek next to his. "Thank you, James," she whispered.

Momentarily, his arms tightened. "No, my love," he said. "It is I who must thank you."

The weeks slipped by in a blaze of sunshine. Catherine regained her strength, and felt her body firming back into shape. She played with and fussed over the baby, and immersed herself in plans for the christening. Davy Aberfan was coming to be godfather, and Catherine was planning a party for all the Allandale servants and tenants.

Allandale drove her in the afternoons, as she was still unable to ride. Catherine loved their drives together, the sound of the horses' hooves, the smell of lilacs, the warmth of the spring sun. They spoke when they felt like it, but often were content with silence. For both it was a period of peace, and they savored the quiet joy they felt in each other's presence. Often their thoughts were so in tune that words were unnecessary. They would simply meet each other's eyes and smile. In the months to come, Catherine often looked back on these weeks of quiet peace with pain-filled nostalgia.

But for the present, nothing appeared to threaten the sun-drenched happiness of her days.

The day of the christening was as beautiful as any hopeful parent could wish. Catherine, Allandale, Sir Francis, Aunt Louisa, and Davy Aberfan all sat down to a festive breakfast as the bright spring sunlight poured in the windows of the family dining room. "Do you know," Catherine said as she helped herself to eggs, "we haven't had a bad day since Eileen was born?"

"That's true," Sir Francis agreed. "It was the love-liest April I can remember, and May looks like it's going to be more of the same. In fact," he added, "I've had several desperate messages from Kate telling me that our farms urgently need my personal attention."

Catherine laughed. "Papa, since when did running the farms become your major occupation?"

Sir Francis cut into his steak. "Since I'm no longer there to agree to whatever everyone plans to do anyway."

"Kate misses you, Papa, that's what it is."

"Well," Sir Francis said reasonably, "she is an excellent housekeeper, but it's hardly fair to ask her to assume responsibility for the entire estate, Cathy."

"I know, Papa."

"You and James and Eileen will have to come and visit me," he continued. "Northumberland is nice and cool in the summer."

"Do you know," Davy said, "it occurs to me that my godchild has blood ties to almost every part of the United Kingdom. The north of England and Scotland from her mother," he gestured toward Catherine, "and southern England and Ireland from her father. It is obvious," he concluded, "that she will have to marry a Welshman."

Catherine laughed and reached out a hand to touch his arm. "She could do worse, Davy."

They all set out for church together, Allandale,

Catherine, the baby, and Aunt Louisa in the chaise, Davy and Sir Francis in the phaeton. Davy watched Allandale as he handed his wife and aunt into the carriage, his daughter deftly tucked in the crook of his arm. "James amazes me," he told Sir Francis, shaking his head. "About the last thing in the world I would have expected from him is that he would be good with babies!"

"Well," Sir Francis said kindly, "this is *his* baby, you know. That makes the difference." But Davy still shook his head in wonder.

As he listened to the words of the baptismal service, Allandale wondered at himself. He had been entirely unprepared for the rush of feeling that had devastated him the first time he held his daughter in his arms. It was a kind of feeling totally new to him, protective and tender, content to lavish itself with little return. Catherine was right when she accused him of doting. But the tiny face of his daughter, her flower-petal skin and clear blue eyes—his eyes as a baby, according to Aunt Louisa—filled him with wonder and delight. It was a love untainted by passion or longing. . . . Irresistibly, his eyes turned to his wife.

Catherine felt him looking at her, but kept her eyes on Aunt Louisa and the baby. "Please, dear God," she prayed, "take away this obstacle that is keeping me from James." Her eyes closed. "Help me, God, please, please help me to find the way. . . ." Her eyes opened and turned to meet his, all trace of inner turmoil carefully removed from her face.

Eileen screamed in protest, and Davy looked alarmed. Aunt Louisa rocked her comfortingly, and the ceremony went on.

"It is a sign of good fortune when they scream, Lady Allandale," the Reverend Mr. Anderson told Catherine as they stood in the bright sunshine in front of the church.

"Well, it's certainly a sign of good lung power," she

returned. "We will see you and Mrs. Anderson at Barton Abbey later?"

"We'll be delighted," he bowed courteously.

Sir Francis took Allandale's place in the chaise on the way home. Davy was delighted to get Allandale alone. "You did a bang-up job on both Castlereagh and Canning, James. That new scheme of Alexander's really shook the old boy, and Canning is pressing the cabinet to formally declare its opposition to England's participation in future European congresses. I understand trouble is brewing in Spain?"

Allandale kept his eyes on the road before him. "Ferdinand has thrown out the constitution of 1812 and has been guilty of the wildest excesses." His gray eyes were veiled by the long lashes. "The men who fought for that constitution are not going to tolerate him much longer. Yes, there will be trouble in Spain."

"And?" Davy gently prodded.

"And, Ferdinand will ask his fellow sovereigns to help him maintain his power, and his throne."

"Christ," Davy ran his hand through his hair. "The same thing is likely to happen in Italy."

"Which is why," Allandale spoke softly, "we must work so that Britain will be the stumbling block in the path of the united 'Christian Sovereigns.' "

Davy fervently agreed. "Are you going to Aix-la-Chapelle, James?"

"Castlereagh asked me to." Allandale frowned. "I might go down to Spain first."

"Good." Davy sounded pleased. "We need all the firsthand information we can get."

The afternoon moved along easily. Allandale and Catherine spent an hour in the ballroom, which had been designated for the reception. They greeted all their servants and tenants, who then drank punch and ate copiously. Later, in the dining room, they entertained Reverend and Mrs. Anderson for dinner.

Catherine wore a new evening dress. It was made of

pale green silk, and was cut low across her breasts. Around her neck she wore Aunt Louisa's emerald pendant. A moment's pause in Mrs. Anderson's flow of conversation as she was engaged in talk by Sir Francis gave Allandale the freedom to look at his wife across the candlelit table. Her hair was swept straight back off her forehead and twisted into a brown coronet high on her head. He thought, as he often had before, that Catherine was the only woman he knew whose beauty could stand that severity of hairstyle. The bone structure of her face was only enhanced by exposure.

The soft light caused her skin to seem luminous. His eyes moved down the exquisite line of her jaw to the emerald pendant. He felt something inside him, quiet these last few months, start to give way. His mouth tightened, and Mrs. Anderson had to repeat her question to him twice.

Later on, in the drawing room, he found he could hardly keep his eyes off Catherine. He had to force himself to the barest imitation of politeness. She was aware of the intensity of his regard. He knew by the way she met his eyes, and winced to see the shadow that crept into her clear gaze. The evening seemed interminable.

As soon as Mr. and Mrs. Anderson had left, Catherine turned to him. "I think I will go to bed. It's been a long day."

With relief, he agreed. At this moment it was torture to be in the same room with her. She moved to the door, tall, slender, infinitely beautiful, infinitely desirable. A brief smile and she was gone. Some of the intolerable tension in Allandale loosened with her departure, and he managed to get through the remainder of the evening with a semblance of composure.

He accompanied Davy and Sir Francis upstairs, then paused in front of his bedroom door. She was so close . . . Too close. He turned and went down the stairs to the library. Mrs. Challoncer was straightening up in the drawing room when Allandale called to her to bring him a couple of bottles of wine.

Catherine was not asleep. Her hearing was always acute, and doubly attuned to Allandale's step. She heard him saying good night to her father and Davy. She heard his hesitation outside his door and his hurried retreat back down the stairs. She lay still, her eyes wide with apprehension. Was it starting again? The desperate need, the anguish of denial? She had allowed herself to hope that he could be content with what they had. They were one in mind and spirit. But, without the other, their closeness was only torture for him.

She had rolled over and buried her face in her pillow. She had given him the one thing in life he lacked: love. And in so doing she had left him bereft. She burrowed deeper and deeper into the pillow, trying to block the anguish of her thoughts.

As the night slowly moved along, Allandale methodically finished one bottle of wine after another. The dawn found him sitting at his desk, head buried in his hands. The wine hadn't helped. The pain was still there.

Carefully he rose and walked toward the door. He mounted the stairs and paused once again outside his room. Eileen slept in Catherine's dressing room, and he could hear her crying and the nurse's attempts to quiet her. He entered his room, looked at his untouched bed, and went to the window. He could hear Catherine moving next door. She was going to the baby. If only he could rid his mind of the suspicion that the reason he had been so pleased with a girl was the deep-buried thought that Catherine would insist on trying to give him a son. He stood without moving as the sun filled the sky and movement began all over the house. Then he changed into his riding clothes and went out again.

The following week was horrible for Catherine. Sir Francis left for Northumberland, and Aunt Louisa went back to London. Only Davy stayed, and he was due to leave also.

The day after the baby's christening, Catherine had made an attempt to conquer her disability. The large front bedroom on the third floor of the house was being prepared for a nursery. Catherine planned to move the baby upstairs very shortly. One of the features of the room was a large cupboard, which she was planning to convert into a small pantry for the use of Eileen's nurse.

The cupboard was untouched as yet, and on the morning after the christening Catherine stood before it. It was large and inside was empty and dark. She could feel the tension mounting inside her as she steeled herself to go in. With grim determination she stepped in and closed the door behind her. Her nails dug into the palms of her hands as she fought for composure. For a moment she thought she had won, then the sense of helpless confinement began to wash over her again. For thirty seconds she held out, then she pushed the door back frantically and tumbled back into the airy, sun-lit room. The whistle of her breath as she desperately sucked air into her lungs was the only sound in the room. For a few moments she was conscious only of the deep relief of escape. Then, as the meaning of her failure became clear, despair swept through her. She put her shaking hands to her face and wept bitterly.

The night before Davy's departure, Catherine watched Allandale's face over dinner. He looked worn out, the very bones of his face bearing the imprint of his fatigue. He had not touched her once all week long.

Davy was saying something about an important government meeting. "I wish you could be there, James."

Catherine said steadily, "Why don't you go up to London with Davy, James?"

His eyes, black with exhaustion met hers. "Leave you and Eileen alone?"

"Don't be ridiculous. This house is crawling with servants. We shall hardly be alone." She saw the resistance in his face, and continued. "I won't be lonely, I promise you. I have the baby and I plan to start training Silverbird."

His lashes veiled his eyes, but a muscle jumped beside his mouth. "I could come back for the weekends."

Smiling, she agreed with him. But they both knew he wouldn't.

XVI

She hath left me here all alone,
All alone as unknown,
Who sometimes did me lead with herself,
And me loved as her own.

—SIR WALTER RALEIGH

Davy knew that something was wrong between Allandale and his wife. It was obvious to any person of moderate sensitivity. What it was, he racked his brains to discover. It had seemed to happen right after the baby's christening. Davy looked at Allandale's profile as he sat beside him in the phaeton on the way to London. It looked like a finely sculptured mask. Davy knew it would be useless to broach the subject that was troubling them both, so he kept to the safer topic of politics.

"I'm glad you're coming to this meeting, James."

"As I'm not officially a member of the government, Davy, I don't know if I'll be coming at all."

"Don't worry." Davy's voice was dry. "Castlereagh is desperate for professional help in the foreign office. You can be invaluable to him, and he knows it. Add to that the fact that Wellington has blasted his approval of you all over London. You'll be invited, all right. And listened to."

An ironic smile pulled at the corners of Allandale's mouth. "I find it irresistibly amusing, Davy. If Castlereagh or Wellington had any idea of my political philosophy, they would have heart palpitations."

Davy laughed. "I'm sure they think that the sixth Earl of Allandale must be a member of the club."

The smile left Allandale's face. "That's the problem with Europe, Davy. Too long a heritage of just the sort of 'club' you're talking about. It is a tradition that will be very difficult to break." He paused for a moment as they negotiated a tricky turn. "In America, they were able to start fresh, but they had no past to break with. I'm afraid Europe isn't going to be able to make it into the modern world without a violent cataclysm."

"The modern world?"

Allandale smiled briefly. "The age of the imperial monarchy is over, Davy. The Holy Roman Empire is gone. The vast Ottoman Empire is on its way out. Napoleon is gone. It may take us another hundred years, but the Hapsburgs and Romanovs will have their day as well."

Davy looked at Allandale curiously. "And the House of Hanover?"

"The British monarchy is a constitutional monarchy. We have the best chance of any European nation of adapting without violence."

"I didn't know you admired America that much."

Allandale sighed. "I envy America. It has none of the burden of history that weighs on us." He looked sidewise at Davy. "Bolívar is doing rather well in South America. One unpleasant blow to Ferdinand would be for England to recognize the independence of the South American nations."

Davy laughed out loud. "James, you fiend! You know that our merchants would be delighted to have us do just that."

"We must mention that aspect of things to Castlereagh," Allandale said smoothly.

The government meeting was held at Lord Castlereagh's London house. Allandale sat silently as one man, then another, offered opinions about the upcoming meeting at Aix-la-Chapelle. Should England agree to commit herself to further fixed meetings of the great European powers? Castlereagh said yes. "It is essential for us to maintain the balance of European power," he argued, "and what better way can we find to ensure that no one nation becomes overly powerful than to exert our influence at a united congress?" He went on, a hint of pride in his voice, "It was due to our exertions at Vienna that no one nation reaped all the spoils of Napoleon's defeat."

"No," Davy's voice was expressionless. "All the smaller nations were very neatly divided up among the major powers."

Canning spoke up. "But what of the Czar's new proposal? He will want us to join a league guaranteeing to each sovereign his throne and his present territory."

Castlereagh frowned. "Of course, we cannot consent to that."

"I'm glad you see that, at any rate." Canning was openly sarcastic.

Castlereagh ignored him. "Lord Allandale," he said, "will you give us your views? You were instrumental in organizing our coming meeting at Aix-la-Chapelle."

Allandale raised his eyes from their contemplation of the table. He looked at the faces turned to him and spoke deliberately. "Our true policy as a nation, gentlemen, has always been not to interfere in European affairs except in great emergencies, and then with a commanding force. This we recently did in the Peninsula." He continued, his voice underlining the meaning of his words. "The people of this country may be taught to look with great jealously for their own liberties if our government is engaged in meetings of great despotic monarchs, deliberating upon what degree of revolutionary spirit may endanger their own security." He looked meaningfully at Castlereagh. "Whatever your personal convictions, my lord, you may find that rebellions, such as those presently brewing in Italy and Spain, might not be unreasonable in the eyes of the English people."

Allandale rose to his feet. "I thank you, gentlemen, for allowing me to join you this evening. And now, having had my say, I will retire and leave you to your deliberations." He bowed briefly and left the room.

There was a moment's silence after the door had closed behind him. Then Sir Alfred Frost looked at Castlereagh. "That was a warning, my lord," he said. "If we want to stay in power, perhaps we had better heed it."

Allandale let Davy drag him to a few parties, and at one of them, inevitably, he met his Aunt Louisa. As she had called once when he was out and he had not returned her visit, she looked somewhat grim as she cornered him.

"How charming to see you, James. I gather your butler failed to inform you of my visit on Friday?"

He looked warily at her. "I knew about it, Aunt Louisa. I'm afraid I've been too busy to come and see you."

"Of course," she agreed affably. "Playing cards at Whites, hanging out at Tattersalls, one can see that your time has been very limited."

His wariness increased. "Have you been having me followed, Aunt Louisa?"

"Of course not, my dear boy. It seems, though, that everyone in London has seen you. Except me."

He made an impatient gesture with his hand. "Oh, all right, Aunt Louisa. I apologize. I should have come to see you."

"Why didn't you?" Her voice was abrupt.

A muscle jumped in his cheek, but otherwise his face was calm. "I imagine you already know the answer to that question, Aunt."

"James," her voice was suddenly gentle. "What is wrong between you and Catherine? I had thought, after the birth of Eileen—I mean you both seemed so happy."

His face was taut. "Leave it, Aunt Louisa."

"How can I see you so unhappy and not try to help?"

"There is nothing you can do," his voice was final. "Now, would you like me to get you a glass of punch?"

Momentarily she accepted the rebuff and, refusing his offer, began to talk of other things.

Lady Lothian next tried Catherine. Catherine's program since Allandale had left mainly consisted in keeping busy. She spent hours outdoors and had just come in from the stables when Aunt Louisa's letter arrived. As Challoncer handed her the missive, the fresh color in her cheeks brightened, but then she looked at the handwriting and knew it wasn't from him. Slowly she opened it and looked first at the signature.

She folded the letter wthout reading it and went upstairs. First she checked in on Eileen, who was napping soundly. The nurse motioned to her to go away and Catherine frowned. She and the nurse were going to have it out very shortly. Catherine did not at all appreciate being made to feel an intruder in her baby's life. "Mrs. Burns," she said softly, "I think your days here are numbered."

Then, having no other delaying tactic she could rely on, she went to her room and opened Aunt Louisa's letter. "My dear child," she read. "I have the greatest aversion to prying, but my love for you and for James forces me to write this. I have seen James several times in the past few weeks, and I am deeply concerned about him. He is far too thin and doesn't look as if he sleeps two hours a night. I know he misses you.

"Why, Catherine, did he leave? Or, if he had to come to London, why could you not have come with him? I know you, and I know you must miss him as much as he does you.

"Come to London, my dear. Believe me, whatever quarrel may have estranged you is trivial beside what you feel for each other.

"Forgive an interfering old woman whose only excuse is that she loves you.—Louisa Caldwell."

Catherine sat for ten minutes, unable to reread the letter because of the tears blurring her vision. Then her eyes focused on the lines that concerned her most, "He is far too thin and doesn't look as if he sleeps two hours a night." Helplessly, she buried her face in her hands. She had desperately hoped it would be better once he got away from her.

Her mind settled into a groove as familiar as it was painful. What could she do? She had made several other unsuccessful attempts to brave out her fear. If she told Allandale she was all right, and the same thing happened again. . . . She remembered the look on his face as he watched her that evening. No, anything was better than that.

"I know he misses you." God knows, she knew that. Weren't her days too filled with the dreadful emptiness of his absence? Everything she laid her eyes on was a reminder. Even her baby . . . Eileen had given her a smile yesterday, full of mischief and delight, and Catherine had found herself averting her eyes. The resemblance was too much to bear.

What to do? What to do? What to do?

First, she must answer Aunt Louisa's letter. She took out a sheet of paper and briefly wrote: "Dear Aunt Louisa, Thank you for your love and your concern. My coming to London would not help. I do not know what I can do." Then, out of her own desperation, she added some lines from Milton:

> "Me miserable! which way shall I fly
> Infinite wrath, and infinite despair?
> Which way I fly is Hell; myself am Hell."

She concluded, "Pray for us."

She took out more paper and wrote another letter, this time to Allandale. Her tone was drastically different from the letter to Aunt Louisa. It was cheerful and newsy, full of stories about the baby and reports on her progress with Silverbird. It was not until the conclusion that another note crept in. "My heart and my thoughts are with you always. We cannot go on like this. I feel it in my soul. The hour of our glory will come."

Allandale read and reread the last lines of her letter. Then he carefully put it in his desk drawer and locked it. The refrain of an old Welsh song ran in his head.

"Gold wears out and silver wears out, but longing never rises from the heart."

He closed his eyes briefly before he moved to the door. He was going to a ball at the Countess of Allmayne's. He didn't want to go, but it was as good a way to pass the evening as any other. What he couldn't face was an evening by himself. "The hour of our glory will come," she had written. *I hope to God I'm alive to see it*, he thought, only half in jest.

Lady Caroline Amberly was at the Countess of Allmayne's ball as well. She and Allandale had met several times previously, and Caroline had been unable to get behind his formal, careful courtesy. Tonight she was determined to break through his reserve.

She stood in the entrance to the ballroom, watching him with hungry eyes. No matter what he wore, Allandale had the knack of looking born in his clothes. He looked as elegant in his old riding breeches as he did in evening dress. Caroline looked jealously at his neatly cut, thick, black hair, the gray eyes so maddening in their remoteness, the long, sensitive mouth belied by the firmness of the chin beneath it. She knew she was looking her best. Her vivid hair fell in graceful ringlets from a knot high on her head. Her low-cut gown of ivory satin emphasized the color of her hair and eyes. Many male eyes watched her appreciatively as she moved gracefully to Allandale's side.

He smiled at her, unshakable courtesy the only expression on his face. "Damn him!" Caroline thought viciously as she returned his smile. "James," she said coaxingly, "I wonder if I might speak to you in private for a moment?"

He looked wary. "In private, Caroline?"

She smiled sweetly. "Please, James? I'm in a bit of trouble and I need your help." She put her hand on his arm and started leading him off the floor. "There is a small anteroom where we can talk."

Allandale let himself be guided by her. Leave it to Caroline, he thought in amusement, to find a room where one can be private.

They entered the anteroom and Caroline swung around to face him. "Why haven't you come to see me, James?"

"Oh God," Allandale groaned, "everyone seems to be asking me the same question."

"Well," she replied with some asperity, "what do you answer them?"

He looked at her steadily. "Why should I come to see you, Caroline?"

Her eyes blazed. "Why? You haven't forgotten what is between us? What passed between us the last time we met?" She began to walk up and down the small room. "Let me refresh your memory, my lord! You held me in your arms, my lord. You made love to me. Then you disappeared into the country with your wife. You go junketing around the world and when you finally do land in London, you barely even speak to me!" Her voice shook and real distress showed in her eyes.

"Oh Christ," he rubbed his eyes tiredly. "What can I say, Caroline? I had told you it was all over between us . . ."

"But then you . . ."

"I know. I know. I never should have gone home with you that night." He looked at her directly. "I had been drinking heavily. You knew that."

"I knew and I didn't care!" she flared. "All I knew was that I loved you." She stopped, then began again more slowly. "I didn't mean to say that, but it is true." She looked at him, her green eyes glistening with tears. "I love you so, James. I have no pride left. Please come back to me."

He looked at her hand lying on his arm. "Caroline, don't . . ."

"Oh God, James! Look at me!" And she flung herself into his arms, her hands drawing his mouth down to hers. For a moment his lips responded to the warmth of hers. But then he drew away.

"Caroline, I'm sorry. God knows," his voice was bitter, "it's irony for me to turn away love. I know too well how painful it is on the other side of the fence."

She walked to the window and reached out to finger the velvet fabric of the drapes. "You love her." It was a statement, not a question.

He answered simply, "Yes."

"But she doesn't love you."

"Catherine feels for me quite as much as I for her."

"Then why have you left her?"

His smile was twisted. "Call it fate. But I have nothing left, Caroline. Catherine has it all."

She came back to him and looked into his face. He met her gaze steadily, his own eyes full of compassion. "Tell her for me she is a fool," she said, and walked out of the room. Allandale slowly followed.

XVII

And wilt thou leave me thus?
That hath given thee my heart,
Never for to depart
Neither for pain nor smart,
And wilt thou leave me thus?
Say Nay! Say Nay!

—SIR THOMAS WYATT

Unknown to Allandale or Catherine, the train of events that was to alter their lives had already been set in motion. Ian Maxwell had returned home before Christmas, angry and bitter. Lord Carberry had listended to his report of all that had passed in London. Then he had shown Ian the letters he had received about Allandale from Lady Lothian and from his old friend General Graham. "I don't say, Ian, that I approve," he said. "It was a havey-cavey affair, the whole thing. But it could be worse."

"Sir!" Ian stared with horror at his grandfather. Lord Carberry was seventy-two years old and only of late had he begun to show it. He was tall and bore himself heroically upright. His mane of hair had long since turned white, but it was still as thick as a boy's. Of late, he had begun to use a stick to walk about with, and when he was angered the bellow of his voice vied with the thumping of his cane.

His eyes, which could flash fiercely, were soft now as they rested on his favorite grandson. "I know, lad. I had the same hopes you did. But," he reached out and gave Ian a pat on the shoulder, "I'm afraid Cathy didn't share them. Francis told me as much when he wrote to say she wasn't coming last summer."

"You never told me that!"

"I know, I know," the old man sighed. "I hoped she'd change her mind. But, Ian lad, what's done is done. We must make the best of it."

Ian's fair face flushed darkly. "I'll never accept it, Grandpapa." He turned on his heel and stalked from the room.

As the weeks and months went by, Ian found his grief and his rage growing. Lord Carberry, whom he had looked to for support, seemed to be totally reconciled to Catherine's marriage. As Ian rode across the stark emptiness of Geordie's Hill, past the bleakness of deserted Hermitage Castle, it seemed as though the world was but a reflection of the emptiness his own life had become.

"Why did she do it? Why did she do it?" the constant refrain beat in his head. For Ian knew what Lord Carberry did not. Catherine wasn't happy. He had seen her strained eyes, her peaked look that told of sleepless nights. Allandale didn't give a damn about her. Anyone could see that.

The early spring had come to Scotland, and with it the news of the birth of Catherine's child. Lord Carberry was thrilled. "A great-grandchild. Too bad it wasn't a boy, but they've plenty of time for that. If she's as bonny as her mother, she won't lack for suitors!"

Ian, however, did some elementary arithmetic, and came up with an interesting conclusion. The date of Catherine's marriage had been July 10. Her baby had been born nine months later, and from what Sir Francis's letter had indicated, she had been well over eight pounds. With his mind revolving one possibility against the other, Ian decided to take a trip to Northumberland.

He told Lord Carberry he was going to visit friends in Carlisle, and set out in early May for Renwick Hall and the town of Haltwhistle. As he drove his curricle along the familiar roads to England, his mind was filled with thoughts of Catherine. The green, sloping country of Liddesdale stretched around him, and every hill, every running burn, was inextricably linked with memories of her. He could almost hear her voice and see the sparkle in her eyes, the fresh color in her cheeks. She had had a story for every inch of landscape he was passing through. Ian's favorite had been the one about the bewildered Roman on guard duty at what must have seemed to him the last outpost of civilization. Catherine had preferred the Border stories told by the old ballads. He closed his eyes briefly and heard her clear voice. His spirits lightened insensibly, and he began to sing himself:

"And have they ta'en him, Kinmont Willie,
    Against the truce of the Border tide?
And forgotten that the bauld Buccleuch
    Is Keeper here on the Scottish side?"

It was going on to dinner time when Ian's bays pulled into the stableyard at The Border Maid. The stableboy came out to take charge of his horse, and Ian walked into the inn. He was met by Mr. Morely, the landlord.

"Mr. Maxwell! How nice to see you, sir."

"How are you, Morely? I was on my way to the Hall and thought I'd stop for a bit of dinner."

"A pleasure, sir, a pleasure." The landlord ushered him into the coffee room and went to see about the fire. "I can give you a saddle of mutton, Mr. Maxwell, and one of Mrs. Morely's chicken pies."

Ian approved this prospective menu, and Mr. Morely withdrew, only to return in a few moments with a glass of sherry. Ian sipped it slowly as the table was laid for his dinner. He had an indescribable feeling that he was close to the mystery of Catherine's marriage, and said to the landlord as his dinner was brought in, "I rather think I will spend the night, Mr. Morely. I don't want to put Kate out by arriving at this late hour at Renwick Hall."

"Very good, sir. I'll tell Mrs. Morely to prepare a room for you." He placed a bottle on the table. "I think you'll like this burgundy, Mr. Maxwell."

Ian ate his dinner slowly, accepting the bottle of port Mrs. Morely brought as the covers were cleared. The landlord's wife had been full of curiosity at Ian's arrival and she seized the opportunity of seeing him. Ian was as pleased to see her.

"Ah, Mrs. Morely. Do sit down and have a glass of wine with me. It's lonesome, dining by oneself."

"Well, Mr. Maxwell," she fluttered, "I don't mind if I do." She accepted the glass Ian poured for her and opened the very topic that was occupying his thoughts. "And how is Miss Renwick—Lady Allandale, that is."

Ian's blue eyes studied her closely. "She has just given birth to a daughter."

Mrs. Morely looked melancholy. "Poor lassie. Sir Francis is still with her, then?"

"Yes, he is staying in Somerset until the christening. Then he will return home. Probably sometime later this week."

Mrs. Morely finished her glass of port. "Poor Lady Allandale will miss him, I'm sure. His presence must have been a great comfort to her."

Ian poured her some more wine. "Please, Mrs. Morely." With a show of reluctance, she accepted it. He spoke carefully. "You seem to have a very negative view of my cousin's marriage."

Mrs. Morely had been remarkably discreet about the events of last July. She genuinely liked the Renwicks and Allandale had paid her handsomely as well. But now, under the influence of the wine and Ian's sympathetic attention, she began to unburden herself. "I must say, sir," she told Ian, "we all thought you and Miss Renwick would make a match of it one day."

"That was my hope also, Mrs. Morely," he returned

steadily. "So you can imagine my distress when I heard that my cousin had married. And married so hastily."

"Aye." Mrs. Morely appeared to hardly notice her glass being refilled. "But it wasna the poor lass's doing, you know."

"Oh?" Ian kept his voice under careful control. He did not want to startle her by betraying the intensity of his interest.

"Yes," Mrs. Morely heaved a sigh. "There was nothing else to do, and so I told Sir Francis."

"You interest me exceedingly, Mrs. Morely. Why was there 'nothing else to do'?"

"Well," she said beginning her fourth glass of wine, "it was plain as a pike what had happened to the poor lassie. The earl, at least, did the handsome thing by her. Good thing, too, as it turned out."

Ian could feel the blood beating in his head. "Are you saying, Mrs. Morely, that the Earl of Allandale seduced my cousin and was forced to marry her by my uncle?"

"Seduced?" Mrs. Morely gave a harsh laugh. "If you could have seen the poor little thing, her clothes ripped off of her, white as a sheet and shaking like she had the ague, you wouldn't say she had been seduced." She looked at Ian and nodded vigorously. "Rape's what we call it in this part of the country, Mr. Maxwell."

Every ounce of color drained from Ian's face. He looked at Mrs. Morely, shock and horror in his eyes. "Catherine was raped by Lord Allandale? And my uncle made him *marry* her?"

Mrs. Morely began to look a little conscience-stricken. "There now, Mr. Maxwell, I shouldn't have told you. I promised both Sir Francis and Lord Allandale." She looked at him doubtfully. "You won't say anything, will you?"

"Don't worry, Mrs. Morely, you have done the right thing in telling me." He rose and escorted her to the door. "No harm will come because of it, I promise you." He forced himself to be quiet and reassuring as she hesitated in the door. When he finally got rid of her, he went to the mantel and futilely pounded his fist against it. His mind filled with images of Cathy, his Cathy, helpless . . . he left the room hurriedly, went out to the courtyard, and was exceedingly sick.

By morning, shock and horror had been replaced by overpowering anger. He had breakfast, served to him by a subdued Mrs. Morely, and drove to Renwick Hall determined to verify her story with Kate.

The housekeeper was surprised and pleased to see Ian. "Mr. Ian!" She ushered him into the house, apologizing for her dress. She had been dusting the books in the library. "I expect Sir Francis back soon, you know. If he can tear himself away from his granddaughter. He sounds positively ecstatic." Ian followed Kate into the front parlor. "I hope Lord Carberry is well?"

Ian answered mechanically. He looked at Kate. Her graying black hair was neatly braided on top of her head. Her old dress was dusty, and there was a smudge of dirt on her cheek. Her round, motherly face was looking at him in inquiry. He knew she was wondering what had brought him to Renwick Hall.

"Kate," his voice was tense, "I know why Cathy married Allandale."

Her face changed. "You do?" she said carefully.

"I had it all last night from Mrs. Morely at The Border Maid. "

"I see." Her hazel eyes looked at him warily. "That wasn't very discreet of her."

"Discreet! What the bloody hell does that mean? Was it discreet to force my cousin into marriage with a man who had done to her what Allandale did?"

"Ian," Kate's voice was calm and reasonable. "It wasn't as bad as you think it was."

"Christ!" he stared at her. "Are you telling me he didn't rape her?"

Her eyes fell. "No, but there were, well, mitigating circumstances."

His eyes were filled with incredulity. "I can't believe

I'm hearing you correctly, Kate. Are you defending him?"

"No, Mr. Ian, I am not defending him. I am simply trying to make you see that, under the circumstances, Sir Francis did the best thing for Miss Cathy."

His voice shook with passion. "By marrying her to such a man? If she had to marry, why did no one think of me? God, at least she would have married someone who loved her!"

"But, Ian, the only reason for the marriage was the possibility of a child. Sir Francis was going to have it annulled otherwise. You couldn't marry a woman who was carrying another man's child."

"Kate!" his voice was filled with anguish. "I would have taken Cathy on any terms. How could you have. . . ." his voice trailed off as words failed him.

She rubbed her temples tiredly. "We weren't thinking very clearly, Ian. Perhaps you're right. But," her voice became more determinedly cheerful, "Sir Francis seems to think the marriage is working out well, so perhaps it was all for the best."

"Oh yes," his voice was harsh, "it's all working out like a dream. I wish, Kate, you could have seen Cathy with her drawn face and tired eyes. It would have warmed your heart." He met her eyes, then, muttered "Oh, hell!" and turned and left the house.

All the way home to Newlands, Ian's brows were furrowed as he tried to find a way to use the knowledge he had just gained. The hills and dales of England, then Scotland, passed unnoticed as he wrestled with his problem. One word Kate had mentioned kept returning to him. Sir Francis had planned to get Catherine an annulment. Considering the circumstances of the marriage, and her age, Ian thought there was a very good possibility that an annulment could still be obtained. He determined to broach the matter with his grandfather when he arrived back home.

He was met at the door, however, by a grave-faced butler. "Mr. Ian, thank God you have returned!"

"What's the matter, Elliott?"

"I'm afraid Lord Carberry has had a stroke. The doctor is just about to leave."

His heart was heavy as Ian listened to the doctor's report. Lord Carberry was gravely ill. According to Dr. McLeod, it was only a matter of time before another stroke killed him.

As Ian looked at the suddenly aged face of his grandfather, tears filled his eyes. The blue eyes, so like his own, opened. "Ian, lad," the strong voice was barely a whisper.

"Grandpapa," Ian took his hand. "You're going to be fine."

Lord Carberry's head shook in a negative. "I'm afraid I've bought it, my boy." He paused, gathering his strength. "I want you to do something for me."

"Anything, Grandpapa."

"Fetch Cathy. And my great-grandchild. I want to see them before," he paused, then made an effort, "before I die."

Ian bent and kissed the old man's hand. "You're not going to die, Grandpapa. But I will bring Cathy and the baby."

"Good boy."

XVIII

Ah, dear, but come thou back to me!
Whatever change the years have wrought,
I find not yet one lonely thought
That cries against my wish for thee.

—ALFRED LORD TENNYSON

The days passed slowly for Catherine. Outwardly, she was busy and contented. But the stress showed in other ways. She never went near the piano anymore. And her milk had dried up. She had been distressed by that, but Dr. Kiley assured her it wasn't all that uncommon. "An emotional disturbance can do it," he said. He looked at her profile. The cameo-pure face with its high-bridged nose and clear-cut lips gave nothing away. He tried a probe. "I expect you miss your husband."

Catherine turned and faced him. "Yes," she said. "Well, can you engage a wet nurse for Eileen?"

He rose. "I have someone in mind, Lady Allandale. I'll send her to see you."

Catherine smiled and accompanied him to the door. "Thank you, you are very kind."

Dr. Kiley stood for a moment looking at her, an expression of fatherly concern on his face. "If you ever need my help," he said brusquely, "don't hesitate to ask."

"Thank you," she said, and let him go.

The lack of music left a huge gap in Catherine's life. For as long as she could remember she had spent hours of her day at the piano. Music was her own special world, her way of giving expression to the emotions that welled up within her. And now that world was closed to her. The emotions she felt were too painful. The only way to survive was to rigidly suppress them.

So Catherine turned to the other main occupation of her childhood—she spent half her day in the stables. The training of the Arabian colt, Silverbird, required enormous time and patience, for which she was deeply grateful. The remainder of the day she spent with her baby.

She was on her way to the stables when Ian arrived. She was coming out the front door of the house wearing her oldest clothes when she saw him pull into the driveway. Astonishment, pleasure, and anger all vied for the premier place in her face. By the time Ian had jumped down and come up the stairs to meet her, she had schooled her expression to one of gracious welcome.

"How nice to see you, Ian. And what a surprise!"

He stood silent for a minute, looking at her. She looked like the old Cathy. Her skin was lightly tanned and her hair was streaked with gold. She stood before him, slender and straight in her old clothes, and he almost wept to see her. Only, as he looked closer, her eyes were not the eyes of the young and carefree girl he remembered.

His voice, when he spoke, was unsteady. "I'm afraid I bring bad news, Cathy."

Her eyes darkened. "Grandpapa?" she asked fearfully.

"Yes. He's alive, but very ill. I would have come sooner, but he had a relapse and I was afraid to leave him."

She roused herself. "Come in, Ian. You must tell me all about it." She gave orders quickly for his chaise to be stabled and wine brought, then led him into a small saloon. She walked with her old swift grace to a chair and waved him to another. "Now," she said intensely, "what has happened?"

"He has had a stroke. The doctor says he can't live long, and he wants to see you." The words were out and for the first time Ian admitted to himself the fact of his grandfather's death. His fair face clenched in unhappiness. He looked at his cousin and saw for a moment not the woman he desired but the girl who had shared his childhood.

"Oh, Ian," her voice broke. "Oh, my dear." In a moment she was beside him, holding him to her. His tears were wet and hot on her breast, and hers dampened his hair. For a moment they were united in grief, as they could never be united in love.

Then she knelt before him and looked into his face. He looked so young and vulnerable and grief-stricken that he hurt her heart. "How long, Ian?"

He shook his head. "We must start immediately."

Challoncer entered the room with the sherry. Catherine poured a glass for Ian and brought it to him. He sipped it and some of the devastation left his eyes. "Where is Allandale?" he said.

"In London." Catherine's tone was calm.

"We can't wait for him."

"I understand that."

"Grandpapa wants to see the baby, too." Ian's voice was difficult.

"I see." Catherine transferred her gaze from him to the window. Her brows contracted. "I shall have to get things organized a bit, Ian. One doesn't just pop a baby in a carriage to make a journey like that."

"No, I guess not."

She came to a decision. "Not tomorrow, Ian. I have too many things to do. But the day after. We can take your chaise and ours as well."

He just nodded, and she went to him again. She rested her hand for a moment on his thick fair hair and said softly, "I know, Ian." She moved to the door. "But right now I'd better get things underway. I'll have Mrs. Challoncer show you to your room." She walked out the door, but it seemed he still could feel her hand on his hair.

The two days he spent at Barton Abbey left little impression on Ian. He hardly saw Catherine except at meals. He had a sense of tremendous activity in the house, and luggage began to pile up in the hallway.

He did remember one thing. Catherine brought him up to the Nursery to see her daughter. He really didn't want to see the baby, but there was no way to avoid it. She lay in her cradle, her small fists waving in front of her face, and when she saw Catherine she laughed. Ian looked quickly at his cousin and the expression in her eyes caused him to clench his jaw. He turned back to the baby.

Eileen was a beautiful child. Her hair had stayed black and sprung like silky down from her small head. Her eyes were beginning to turn gray, and the lashes that framed them were astonishingly long and dark. There was nothing of Catherine in her: She was the image of her father. Ian said "She's lovely," in a choked voice.

Catherine smiled at him radiantly. "Isn't she marvelous?" She bent over the cradle and gently chucked Eileen under her chin. "How's Mama's little love?" The baby gurgled and Catherine looked gratified. "She's a very happy baby," she told Ian. "I hope she stays that way after being jounced in a chaise for hundreds of miles." She kissed the baby's silky head and led him out of the room. "I must go to the kitchen and see about getting some jars of fruit packed." She pushed a strand of hair out of her face. "Why don't you go for a ride, Ian?" And he did.

Finally, they were on their way. Things had not fallen out exactly as Ian had planned. He had determined to tell Catherine of his own enlightenment about her marriage and beg her to let him try to get her an annulment. He had envisioned Catherine and himself alone in the carriage as they travelled across England. She would have to listen to him. She would have to agree to his proposal.

He hadn't counted on the baby. Catherine, the wet

nurse, and Eileen rode in one chaise, Ian and the mountains of luggage in the other. When he had suggested to Catherine that she might ride with him for a little, she had looked at him as though he were a madman. "Eileen still doesn't know Mrs. Johnson all that well. This is so disrupting for her, poor love. Her schedule is all shot to pieces. Of course I can't leave her."

That damn baby, Ian thought viciously. She had thoroughly fouled up his plans. And he had a dreadful suspicion that more trouble lay ahead because of her. Catherine may have married James Pembrook because she had been forced to. But it was obvious to the meanest intelligence that she adored his baby. After two days of travel, two days of watching Catherine efficiently subjugate all the needs of everyone else to the needs of her child, Ian had no doubt that the only way he was ever going to get Catherine would be to acquire the baby as well.

He was not so sure about that. An annulment would mean the marriage never existed. Legally that must surely mean the child belonged to her mother? The more he thought about it, the more Ian convinced himself that there should be no problem with Catherine's keeping her child at the same time that she shed her husband. If the child were a boy, things might be different. Allandale, however, obviously cared for his daughter as little as he cared for his wife. He would let Catherine keep the child. Ian decided it would be a politic idea to start to show some interest in what was obviously the light of Catherine's life.

Catherine remained totally oblivious to the plots and plans that were seething in Ian's brain. His unhappy look she put down to his concern for their grandfather. He was tremendously helpful at all their stopovers, seeing to rooms and horses with efficiency. And to Catherine's deep gratification, he began to take an interest in Eileen. She thought, hopefully, that perhaps he was becoming reconciled to her marriage after all.

And so, in outward harmony, they arrived at Newlands. As they had approached the north of England, Catherine felt her spirits, unaccountably, begin to lift. She was deeply worried about her grandfather, concerned for her baby, in despair over her husband, but as the carriage moved out of Carlisle and across the Scottish border, the familiar rough hills and rushing waters lightened the burden on her heart. "Look, lovey," she said to the baby, and held her up to look out of the window. "Isn't it beautiful?"

The nurse looked out at the bleak, empty scenery. There were no houses, no gardens, no fields. Only heather and rough grass, and hills stretching around on all sides. She thought of the neat, cultivated landscape of her home county and shook her head. Lady Allandale was obviously mad.

As they approached closer and closer to their destination, Ian felt the fear he had been trying to bury flood through him. If they were too late? If he were never to see his grandfather again? Catherine's thoughts were a duplicate of his and when the two chaises pulled up in front of the big square stone house, they alighted and moved together for mutual support. The old butler opened the door and his worn face lightened at the sight of them. "Mr. Ian! Miss Catherine!"

Ian spoke, his voice tight, "Then, we're not too late?"

Elliott opened the door wider. "No, Mr. Ian. Lord Carberry's still very ill, but his condition hasn't worsened."

The cousins looked at each other, and the relief in Ian's eyes was echoed in Catherine's. She turned to Elliott. "I think, then, I will take the time to freshen up a bit before I see him." She turned and lifted the baby from Mrs. Johnson's arms.

Elliott's face beamed as he looked at Eileen. "You're in your old room, Miss Catherine, and we've put the bairn next door." He smiled at the baby, who was yawning herself awake from a comfortable nap. "That's a sight will cheer his lordship up!"

A half an hour later, Catherine tapped softly at the door of Lord Carberry's room. His voice, much fainter than she remembered, called "Come in!" She opened the door and stood for a moment on the threshold, trying to overcome her shock. He had aged twenty years. "Lass!" His voice, full of gladness, reached her and with a warm smile she moved across the room. She bent and kissed him and, on the bed next to him, gently placed his great-grandchild.

The only thing unchanged about Lord Carberry was his eyes. They were as bright and fierce as ever, but they softened remarkably as he looked from Eileen to Catherine. "She must look like her father," he said.

Catherine laughed. "The spitting image."

Lord Carberry was silent for a moment, a look of contentment on his face. Then he roused himself. "Where's Ian?"

"Here I am." Ian came to the other side of the bed. "It's good to see you, sir." His voice wavered a moment, then became stronger. "Didn't I tell you I'd get Cathy here?"

"Yes," the old man smiled, "you did." Then he looked at the door again. "But where is your husband, child?"

Catherine's clear gaze never wavered. "He was in London when Ian came, Grandpapa. He is working with the government on this upcoming international congress."

"Oh." The shrewd old eyes surveyed her face. "I was angry with you, lass. Marrying on the sly like that."

"I know. I'm sorry, Grandpapa. But you will like James, I'm sure of that."

He nodded and suddenly looked tired. "Well, I'll see you all later. Just now, I think I'll take a little rest."

"Of course, Grandpapa." Catherine picked up the baby and kissed him again. "It's so good to see you again."

Ian had moved to the door with her, when Lord Carberry called him. He moved back to the bed and looked at the sunken face of his once-vigorous grandfather. Lord Carberry held out his hand. "Thank you, lad." Ian bent and kissed his hand, unable to speak. He left the room with Catherine.

They stood outside his closed door and looked at each other, their young faces stricken. "Oh, Ian," Catherine whispered, "he looks terrible."

He nodded, his throat working. "I know. I'm going to ride into town to see the doctor."

"Yes. I think you should." She stood and watched his blond head as he went down the stairs, then buried her face in the softness of her baby.

XIX

Thou wrong'st a gentleman who is as far
From thy report as thou from honor, and
Solicit'st here a lady that disdains
Thee and the Devil alike.

—WILLIAM SHAKESPEARE

The doctor's report brought no comfort to Lord Carberry's grandchildren. It was just a matter of time, he said. He had engaged a competent nurse to make sure Lord Carberry's needs were taken care of. But besides making sure that he was clean and comfortable, there was little anyone could do.

Catherine wrote to her father and asked him to come. She also wrote to her husband. She told him where she was, and why. But she did not ask him to come.

Allandale was out of town when her letter arrived. He had taken a quick trip to Spain, and had written to Catherine at Barton Abbey to inform her of his whereabouts. His letter arrived the day she left and was not forwarded.

Sir Francis left for Scotland immediately. He was somewhat wary of meeting Ian after what Kate had told him. But he genuinely loved his father-in-law and he knew his daughter would be deeply distressed by his death. So he went.

Ian and Catherine had quickly fallen into a routine which Sir Francis's arrival did not disturb greatly. Lord

Carberry was not up to much conversation, but he clearly found the presence of his grandchildren a deep comfort. Catherine and Ian took turns sitting with him. Her free time Catherine spent with Eileen.

After dinner, Sir Francis would go up to sit for an hour or so with Lord Carberry and Ian and Catherine sat alone in the drawing room. The weather had changed since they arrived, and it was cold and rained most of the time. In the evening, with the fire giving off warmth, they would sit quietly, listening to the sound of the rain against the window.

They both looked forward to this quiet time together. There was room now for nothing between them but their mutual care for an old man they both loved. Only they could truly understand the loss that threatened them both. And both felt less lonely and bereft in each other's company.

They spoke little, and when they did it was always of the past. The last year with its bitter heritage of love offered and love rejected was wiped away. For this period of time they were just Ian and Cathy, Lord Carberry's favorite grandchildren.

Day by day the old man failed. He had spells when his breathing was labored and difficult. Yet he was in no pain and seemed to be at peace. "It's his heart," the doctor told them. "It was damaged in the last attack and is under severe stress now. It will just give out one of these days."

One day Lord Carberry opened his eyes from one of the dozes that overtook him continually. Ian was sitting with him and was, for a moment, unaware of his grandfather's gaze. "Don't look so tragic, lad," the frail voice said with surprising clarity.

Ian moved swiftly from the window where he had been standing. He stood beside his grandfather's bed and smiled with difficulty. "I'm worried about you, Grandpapa."

Lord Carberry's eyes burned with some of their old fierceness. "I've had a good life, lad. I've nothing to regret. But everyone's time comes, someday. No point in lingering beyond it." He paused and looked closely at the young face before him. "Don't grieve for me overmuch, lad. Get on with the business of life." He reached out a hand and Ian took it in his warm grasp. "Will you do that for me, Ian?"

Ian bit his lip, but the bright eyes of his grandfather held his. "Yes, Grandpapa," he whispered.

"Good boy." Lord Carberry's eyes closed, then opened again. He said, surprisingly, "Live your own life, my boy. And let your cousin live hers." This time his eyes closed and stayed shut.

Ian stayed still for a moment, then quietly left the room. He met Catherine in the hall and told her he was going out for some air. She nodded. "I'll go sit with him."

It was a gray, dreary day, but so far the rain had held off. Ian took a horse from the stables and headed northwest toward the deserted Hermitage Castle. The clouds were hanging so low they almost touched the hills. Ian dismounted at the bleak old fortress, for so many years a bulwark against English invasion. Its look of desolation matched Ian's mood. Leaving his horse, he moved inside the grim stone fortress. He looked up and saw the heavy, hanging sky.

With an abrupt motion, he sat on a pile of stone and buried his head in his hands. His grandfather's words echoed around his brain. "Get on with the business of living . . . let your cousin live hers." But grandpapa didn't know the truth behind Catherine's marriage. And *he* did. It had been pushed to the back of his mind these past few weeks, but he had not forgotten.

The question was, what should he do about it? Catherine had not once mentioned Allandale to him. She had received no letter from him, that he knew of. It only confirmed his opinion of their marriage. His own estrangement from her seemed a thing of the past. Surely, Ian thought desperately, she would listen to him. He determined, at the first opportunity, to put his fate to the touch.

When he arrived back at Newlands, Catherine herself met him at the door. She was pale and the strain they had all been under for the past few weeks showed clearly in her face. "Ian," her voice quivered. "Dr. McLeod is with Grandpapa. I'm afraid. . . ." He put an arm around her and they both walked to the staircase. The doctor was just coming down. Sir Francis was with him. Sir Francis spoke gently.

"It is all over. He just slipped away quietly, in his sleep."

Catherine spoke, her voice still not steady. "I was sitting with him, and he seemed to be sleeping as usual. He was breathing—I saw the covers rise and fall. Then I picked up a book and read a few pages. When I looked up again, he looked—strange, somehow. I went over and he didn't seem to be breathing anymore."

Ian's arm tightened around her. "I think he knew the end was near. He told me," he paused, then went on, "he told me not to grieve for him."

Sir Francis looked at the two stricken young faces and began to gently shepherd them toward the drawing room. The doctor indicated that he would make all the necessary arrangements, and left them alone. Sir Francis saw him to the door and returned to the drawing room.

"It was best this way," he said. "He would have hated to linger on, an invalid. He lived all his life in the full vigor of health. It was a long life and a good one." His eyes were on Ian. There was a look on the boy's face that made Sir Francis fearful. Catherine had her baby. She also had, one assumed, a husband. The loss of her grandfather was a grief, but one she would get over.

Ian was a different matter. He had been devoted to Lord Carberry, Sir Francis knew. This loss, coming on top of the loss of Catherine . . . Sir Francis remembered what Kate had told him of Ian's behavior, and looked at him with great concern. He quoted, more for Ian's sake than for Catherine's:

Nothing is here for tears, nothing to wail Or knock the breast, no weakness, no contempt, Dispraise, or blame, nothing but well and fair, And what may quiet us in a death so noble.

"He died in no pain and great peace, with those he loved about him. No man may wish for more."

Ian saw the concerned look in Sir Francis's eyes and managed a smile. "Thank you, Uncle Francis. I'll try to remember that."

Lord Carberry's funeral was held three days later. Catherine thought that half of Liddesdale must have turned out. The small kirk was crowded with relatives and friends, but outside the street was lined with the common people to whom Lord Carberry had been such a terror, and such a good friend. For more than half a century he had reigned over Liddesdale with almost feudal authority; his death saw the end of a way of life.

The heavy skies had lifted, and as the funeral cortege left the church the sun broke through. Catherine walked with Ian, his hand clasped firmly in hers. All through that day and the days that followed, as she played hostess to the Maxwells who thronged the house, one thought remained ever-present in her heart. Where was Allandale?

The house had emptied of relatives, leaving Ian—now Lord Carberry—Sir Francis, and Catherine. In some distress, she approached her father. "I think, Papa, I shall return to Renwick Hall with you."

"Wonderful, Cathy." He scanned her face. "You've had no word from James?"

"No." She bit her lip. "It isn't like him at all, Papa. I think, instead of returning to Somerset, I'd like to stay with you until I hear from him." Her voice was calm, but her eyes were deeply troubled.

Sir Francis didn't pursue the matter. "It will be a pleasure to have you, Cathy. Kate is dying to see Eileen!" She smiled, but her heart wasn't in it.

Later that afternoon, Catherine and Ian went for a ride. She had on the old pair of Ian's riding breeches that she always wore in Scotland. As they swung into their saddles, she turned to him, gaiety in her voice. "It's marvelous to ride astride again."

He knew how sidesaddle had always irked her, and looked at her curiously. "In London you can't, of course. But surely you can ride as you please in the country?"

She looked rueful. "Lady Allandale, I fear, occupies a far more exalted position than mere Miss Renwick." She flashed Ian a look, then grinned. "In truth, Ian, I didn't have the nerve."

He looked skeptical. "I can't believe that, Cathy." The open moor lay before them. The smell of wet moss and bog water was in their nostrils. It was their favorite place for a gallop, and the horses leaped forward in unison.

Catherine sat, poised and lithe in the saddle, her spirit rejoicing in the freedom and speed. The wild gallop across her beloved moors and rolling hills brought for a moment release from the strain of the last few weeks. But, as they slowed the horses down to a canter, then a trot, reality came rushing back. Ian rode quietly beside her, quick to take in the changing expressions on her face. Watching her, so beautiful in her gravity, he felt a fresh pain tighten about his heart, remembering her face after other gallops, turned with such ardent pleasure to his.

He took a firm grasp on his courage, and spoke. "Let's sit down by the burn over there, Cathy. I want to talk to you."

She agreed. "I want to talk to you, too." When they had dismounted and were sitting side by side on a wide rock facing the running water, she spoke first. "I'm going back to Northumberland with Papa, Ian. We'll be leaving in a day or two."

Ian kept his eyes on the water, sparkling in the bright sun. "Does this mean you aren't going back to him?"

With an effort she kept her voice serene. "No. It simply means that Eileen and I are going to visit Papa for a while."

"I see." He turned and looked at her profile, so clear in the brilliant light of the morning. "Cathy, I know why you married him."

Startled, her eyes swung around to him. "What do you mean?"

"I had the whole story from Mrs. Morely at the Border Maid."

Her eyes were clear, the golden light of the day reflected in them. "I see." Then, as the implications of what he had said began to register, a hint of anger came into her voice. "What ever caused you to go snooping around behind my back, Ian?"

"Cathy!" His voice was astonished. "What a thing to say to me. I 'snooped,' as you choose to call it, because I love you and it seemed to me you were desperately unhappy. Don't you see," he pleaded, "I had to find out why you did it?"

She closed her eyes briefly. "I suppose you did."

"Listen to me, Cathy," his voice was urgent. "You don't have to continue with this farce of a marriage. I don't know why the hell Uncle Francis pushed you into it in the first place!" He grabbed her hand, and she let him have it. "We can get it annulled, I know we can. Then you can marry me. And as for Eileen," his words were rushing out, falling over one another in his eagerness, "she'll belong to you. And I'll love her. I do love her!" He looked at his cousin's still face. "Will you, Cathy?"

For a long moment she was silent, her eyes on their clasped hands. Then, slowly, she disengaged her fingers and linked her hands around her knee. Her low-pitched voice, when she spoke, was gentle but final. "No, Ian. I will not."

"In God's name, Cathy, why?"

"I told you the answer to that once, Ian, and you didn't believe me. Now I'll tell you again. What you found out was true. I did not marry James Pembrook because I wanted to. But I shall stay married to him." She looked him full in the face, and absolute conviction was in her voice. "I love him, Ian, as I shall never love anyone else. He is more to me than life. And I shall never change."

He took her by the shoulders, and the grip of his fingers bit into her flesh. "How can you tell me that, Cathy? He doesn't love you. *I* love you!" In his frustration, he shook her.

She didn't answer, but looked at his hands on her shoulders. Slowly he released her. "James loves me, Ian. It would probably be better for him if he didn't. But, God help him, he does."

"I don't believe you."

She rose to her feet. "If you don't believe a word I say, there is obviously no point in continuing this conversation." She moved swiftly to her horse and, standing on a log, remounted. "I'll see you back at the house."

He stood listening to the receding hoofbeats, his nails digging hard into his palms. The tremendous emotional blow of his grandfather's death had left him unprepared to deal with this fresh bereavement. His hands shook as he picked up the reins of his horse. "I won't let her go," he said aloud. Then, desperately, "I can't let her go." He rode home slowly, revolving in his mind a blossoming plan of action.

XX

Yet love that all thing doth subdue,
Whose power there may be life eschew,
Hath wrought in me that I may rue
These miracles to be so true,
  That are impossible.
                    —SIR THOMAS WYATT

Allandale returned to London and found Catherine's letter awaiting him. He frowned and went off in a black mood to see his Aunt Louisa. He was ushered into her presence immediately. "James!" she was clearly agitated, "thank God you have returned."

He kissed her cheek, but his expression did not soften. "I just got back and found a four-week-old letter from Catherine. What's all this about Lord Carberry?"

The expression on Aunt Louisa's face aged her ten years. "He is dead, James. I just had a letter from Catherine myself. They buried him last week."

He looked at his aunt and his voice became more gentle. "I'm sorry, Aunt Louisa. I know you will miss him."

She paused, then said simply, "Yes, I shall. I'm sorry you never met him."

"What I want to know," his voice was harsh again, "is why the hell I never heard from Catherine while I was in Spain?"

"I don't think she knows where you were, James."

"What?"

"In her letter she asked me to tell you of Alexander's death. Evidently, she assumed you were still in London, and that I would be seeing you."

His black brows were drawn together. "I wrote to tell her . . . wait. I wrote to Barton Abbey. Surely the fools there forwarded my letter!"

Aunt Louisa regarded him, eyebrows raised. He was very tan, and his pale gray eyes looked more astonishing than ever in their black-lashed frames. His mouth was taut and a pulse was beating in his temple. "I suggest, James, she said dryly, "you get yourself to Scotland in a hurry. Your wife and daughter are at Newlands and, from what I can see, they must think you're simply ignoring them."

"Don't be ridiculous," he snapped. "Catherine knows better than that."

"Does she?" Aunt Louisa sounded skeptical.

Allandale swore and turned on his heel. "I'll leave immediately."

The door slammed behind him, but Aunt Louisa still stood in the middle of the room. "I have a feeling," she said to the china dog on the table, "that something good is going to come out of all this."

Two days after Catherine's conversation with Ian, she was packed and ready to go. Sir Francis delayed their departure, however. He was an executor of Lord Carberry's will. "I'm afraid I'm going to have to go into Hawick to see the lawyers, Cathy," he told his daughter. "I'd just as soon get it over with and not have to make the trip from Northumberland." She agreed to wait another day.

Catherine had said nothing to her father about her conversation with Ian. But Sir Francis knew something must have happened between them. They no longer acted like the comrades they had been of old. Ian's eyes when he looked at Catherine held an expression that made Sir Francis acutely uncomfortable. He determined to remove her as soon as possible to Renwick

Hall. And, unknown to Catherine, he wrote a letter to Allandale.

He left for Hawick the next day, planning to return that evening. He had been gone about an hour when Ian, his face frightened and distressed, sought Catherine out. She was in the baby's room and turned when he called her name. One look at his white face brought her to his side.

"Ian! What's happened?"

He swallowed, then handed her a letter. "This just came for you, Cathy. I'm afraid something's happened to Allandale. . . ."

She ripped the letter from his hand and tore it open. Its message was brief: "Come quick. James has been injured and is asking for you. —Louisa Caldwell." Every ounce of color drained from her face.

"Who brought this?" she said tensely.

"Someone from Carfrae Castle."

But when the boy was brought to her, he could tell her nothing. He thought "the lord" had fallen from a horse, but he "wasna just sure." Catherine couldn't believe that Allandale could have taken such a serious fall, but the boy was no help. All he knew was that he had been told to deliver the letter.

Catherine resolutely forced herself to think only of the ride that faced her, not about what she would find at Carfrae. He isn't dead, she thought to herself. I would know if he were. She turned to Ian. "Can you send someone with me?"

"Don't be silly, Cathy." His voice was harsh. "I'll go with you. You'll want to leave immediately?"

"Yes. I'll tell Eileen's nurse, and leave a message for Papa."

"Pack your things. I'll see about the carriage."

She shook her head. "No, Ian. Let's ride. We can cut across country some of the way. We'll save miles."

"It's almost two hundred miles!"

She spoke adamantly. "I don't care. I'll pack a few things in a saddle bag."

He hesitated a moment, then gave in. "All right. Change your clothes. I'll see about the horses."

In exactly twenty minutes they were ready to set off. Catherine wore boots and Ian's old breeches. Before she mounted, she briefly covered his hand with hers. "Thank you, Ian, for going with me." He gave her an odd look but said nothing. He simply held his locked hands out to boost her into the saddle.

They rode north, the towering bulk of Cauldcleuch Head behind them, the sweep of moors before them. They turned off the road and headed across the rolling hills of the open border country, across burns and bogs, the sound of their horses' hooves the only disturbance in the clear day. They made it to St. Boswells, but then Ian insisted they stay on the main road. "It's getting late," he said. "I don't want to get caught in the hills by the dark."

Catherine agreed, one of the few times she had spoken since they started. As they pushed on to Oxton the sky, which had been clear save for a few high, white clouds, began to darken with rain clouds. Catherine was tired. Her mind, grateful for something else to think about, concentrated on her exhaustion.

By the time they reached Oxton it was dark. "There's an inn here where we can stop, Cathy." Ian said. "We can't go any further tonight. We're at least forty miles from Carfrae. We'd only get lost in the hills if we tried to go on." He looked at her more closely. "Besides, you're exhausted."

Wearily, she agreed to stop. "But I want to start out with the first light, Ian." He agreed.

Catherine didn't think she would sleep, but physical exhaustion could not be denied. She slept deeply, and woke as the sky began to lighten in the morning. The clouds still hung heavy. It looked as though it was going to rain before long. Catherine dressed and tucked the night dress she had brought back into her saddlebag. She washed her face, combed her hair, and went along to knock at Ian's door. He answered her call and she went down to the coffee room.

Over breakfast they discussed the route they would take. Carfrae Castle was northeast of Oxton. To get there they would have to cross the Lammermuir Hills. Ian was talking about landmarks and things, but Catherine suddenly found she couldn't concentrate on what he was saying. He seemed to be very far away. She made a great effort to focus her eyes on his face but failed. "I must be more tired than I thought," she heard her voice say. Then everything went black.

Ian looked at the brown head resting on the table, the expression in his eyes an odd mixture of pain and determination. "I'm sorry, Cathy," he said. He reached out and gently touched her hair. She didn't stir. Rising, he went out and had the coach he had hired the night before brought around. He lifted Catherine and carried her outside. No one asked any questions. He had paid them too well. Catherine was gently put into the carriage and Ian took the driver's seat. In ten minutes they had pulled out of the courtyard and were heading for the coast.

When Sir Francis returned from Hawick, he discovered the household in a turmoil. "Lord Allandale has been taken ill and Mr. Ian and Miss Catherine went to see him," he was informed by Elliott before he even crossed the threshold.

"Allandale ill?" Sir Francis looked very surprised.

"Ill or hurt, Sir Francis."

"How did you hear this?"

"A boy came from Carfrae Castle this morning, Sir Francis. Mr. Ian, Lord Carberry I should say, and Lady Allandale left right away."

Sir Francis frowned deeply as he pulled off his gloves. "Did anyone else go with them?"

"No, Sir Francis. Oh, Miss—Lady Allandale left a letter for you."

"Well, for heaven's sake, give it to me!" Sir Francis looked at the old butler in exasperation. But Catherine's letter shed no more light on the mystery. She simply wrote that she had gotten an urgent summons from

Lady Lothian to tell her that James was injured and was asking for her. She asked him to stay with Eileen until she knew more definitely what had happened.

Sir Francis had a very uneasy feeling about the whole business. If he had a drop of Celtic blood in him, he would have said he was "fey." As it was, he couldn't shake the feeling that something was dreadfully wrong. If Allandale were at Carfrae, why had he sent Catherine no word? Sir Francis had a very good idea as to what was wrong with the marriage, and his sympathy extended to both parties. But he didn't think Allandale would deliberately cut off all communication with Catherine. And he was most definitely disturbed about Ian.

"I don't like this," he muttered to himself as he went in to dinner. "I don't like this at all." For the moment, however, he didn't see what he could do. Tomorrow he would send someone to Carfrae.

Elliott appeared halfway through dinner and said "Sir Francis!" in a shaken voice. He turned to the door and Allandale followed the old man into the room.

"James!" Sir Francis was so surprised he knocked over his glass of wine.

Allandale looked genuinely puzzled. "What is the matter, sir? From my reception one would think I was a ghost come back from the dead." He surveyed the room, then his eyes returned to Sir Francis. "Where is Catherine?"

Sir Francis looked appalled. "I knew it!" he said. "I knew there was something wrong."

Allandale looked like he was trying to keep a tight rein on his temper. "Sir," his voice held suppressed violence, "will you kindly tell me what the bloody hell you are talking about. And," he spoke slowly and clearly, "*where is my wife?*"

"Sir down, James. I don't know where she is."

Allandale remained standing, but moved closer to Sir Francis. He had seen his father-in-law this upset just once before. Looking at the distinguished face before him, he began to realize that something was very wrong indeed. He sat down. "You'd better tell me," he said briefly.

In reply, Sir Francis handed him Catherine's letter. Allandale read it, his brows contracted. His gray eyes, dark with apprehension, met Sir Francis's. "What does this mean?"

Sir Francis stared down at the red stain his wine had left on the tablecloth. "It's Ian, I think." He frowned. "I don't think he's in a very healthy state of mind, James. He's a deeply sensitive boy. He was distraught over losing his grandfather. And I doubt if he's thinking very clearly about Cathy."

"Catherine has been married now for a year."

"I know." Sir Francis's blue eyes met the steady ones of his son-in-law. "I don't think Ian has ever accepted Cathy's marriage to you. He—" Sir Francis hesitated, then resolutely went on, "he made a trip to Northumberland and managed to discover all the gory details. He had quite an interview with my housekeeper." His gaze dropped from Allandale's rigid face to the stained tablecloth. "Apparently he has convinced himself that Cathy is miserable and is only keeping to the marriage because of the baby."

Allandale's voice was harsh. "Has he spoken to Catherine about this?"

Sir Francis sighed. "I think so. They were getting along famously—quite like old times. Then all of a sudden Cathy froze up with him. She was very anxious to leave for Northumberland." He paused, then went on, "I was in Hawick today to see Lord Carberry's lawyer. He mentioned to me that Ian had been asking him about annulment procedures."

Allandale's face was unreadable. "I see. He asked her to get an annulment, then. And she refused."

"I'm sure that's what happened. But Ian is on the edge, James. I'm very afraid that what he couldn't get one way, he means to get another."

"In effect, he has kidnapped her." Allandale's eyes were black, but his voice remained steady. "Where would he take her, sir?"

Sir Francis ran his fingers through his hair. "Let me think." He paused, then jumped to his feet. "I'll be right back."

By a major effort of will, Allandale retained his control. But it seemed hours until Sir Francis returned. "I've been questioning the servants. I think I know where they're going. St. Abb's."

"Where?"

"St. Abb's. It's on the North Sea, between Dunbar and Berwick-upon-Tweed. There's a castle there that belonged to Ian's mother. It's a wreck, but Ian had a small house built there. It's where he keeps his boat." Sir Francis looked very distressed. "I'm afraid he's going to try to leave the country."

"He won't make it." Allandale took the map Sir Francis handed him and spread it out. "He has Catherine fooled, so he'll have to pretend they're heading for Carfrae. It should pull them out of their way. I'll head straight for the coast." He folded the map. "I'll catch them."

Sir Francis looked at his son-in-law's face and was afraid. "I don't think he's really responsible, James," he said.

"If he touches her," Allandale said evenly, "I'll kill him."

Allandale had several hours of daylight left, and he took advantage of them. Holding his horse to a steady canter, he too headed across the open country. He determined to make Jedburgh by dark, but was in open country when he lost daylight. The sky was overcast, so he had no moonlight to guide him. Allandale, however, was no stranger to this kind of travel, and his uncanny instinct for direction brought him safely to Jedburgh. In Jedburgh he changed horses and from there he held to the road. By early morning he was in Kelso, and by then he was having trouble staying in the saddle. He had been traveling for almost twenty hours, the last hours at a brutal pace. And he had been exhausted to begin with. He knew if he were to be of any use to Catherine he would need a few hours' sleep. He decided to give himself three hours, and woke up the landlord of the Blue Boar in Kelso. Actually, it was four hours before he was in the saddle again.

During the remainder of the ride, Allandale changed horses once. He was held up for an hour when his horse threw a shoe outside of Coldstream and had to be walked to town. It took him a precious half-hour to locate a suitable replacement in Coldstream, and by the time he turned north for the coast he was shaking with temper and fear. Finally, in the early afternoon, the wind began to smell of salt. He pressed his tired horse even harder; the sky opened and rain poured down. With brutal determination he began the short trip that would take him to St. Abb's.

XXI

But love is a durable fire
In the mind ever burning,
Never sicke, never old, never dead,
From itself never turning.

—SIR WALTER RALEIGH

Catherine awoke. Nausea threatened to overcome her, and for a few moments she lay with closed eyes. Slowly she opened her eyes again and breathed slowly and deeply. She swung her feet to the floor and looked around her in bewilderment. She was sitting on a narrow bed in a small, sparsely furnished room. She walked to the front window and looked out. The North Sea rolled up in gray, tossing waves. To her right, anchored in the sheltered bay, was a medium-sized yacht. Catherine recognized it immediately, and a dreadful suspicion began to creep into her mind. She tried the door and it was locked. Anger such as she had never known began to take possession of her. With shaking hands she went back to sit on the bed and wait for Ian.

He came in twenty minutes. When he saw she was awake he stopped, then came forward warily. "How do you feel, Cathy?"

Her voice was icy. "Sick. And I have a headache. Will you kindly explain to me what I am doing here? Where is James?"

"I don't know where he is, Cathy. I'm sorry I had to fool you with that phony letter. But it was the only way I could think of to make you come with me."

"I see. And what did you give me to put me to sleep?"

"A sleeping draught in your coffee this morning. I asked Dr. McLeod for it—told him I couldn't sleep." His blond hair was disordered and hectic color flared in his cheeks. "I had to do it, Cathy. I can't let you go." He looked at her as she sat on his bed. Her hair had come loose and hung like pale brown silk to her waist. Her eyes were as gray and stormy as the day, her skin as beautiful as Eileen's. With a blind look in his eyes, he moved toward her, his voice husky and unsteady. "I love you, Cathy. I want you more than anything in the world." He pulled her to him and his lips came down on hers.

Ian's mouth was hard and seeking. There was no gentleness in his hands as he crushed her to him. But none of the symptoms of suffocation besieged Catherine now. She felt no fear. There was room in her for only one emotion—burning, flaming anger. She struggled to free herself from his grasp and when she failed, she swung back her booted foot and smashed him as hard as she could in the shin. He winced in pain and his grasp loosened. Catherine put the length of the room between them.

"How dare you!" Her eyes literally flashed sparks at him. "Who the hell do you think you are, Ian Maxwell? And what in the name of God do you think you're doing?"

There was a queer lack of focus in his eyes, but he replied calmly enough. "I am taking you to France, Cathy. We'll send a letter to Allandale and say you want an annulment. Under the circumstances, I think he'll be glad to give it to you."

The fierce, strong anger still burned in Catherine's veins. "How lovely. You neglect to mention just one thing, Ian. If you do this, I will hate you all my life."

The strange, blind look never left his eyes, and he made a gesture oddly like that of a sightless man. "That's a chance I'll just have to take," he said in a low voice. "We leave in an hour." He left the room and locked the door behind him.

Catherine tried it anyway and found it wouldn't give. Her mouth set in grim determination as she went to the window that did not look out on Ian's boat. It was not locked, but she was at least twenty feet from the ground. The house was built on a cliff overlooking the sea, and the drop from her window to the steep rocks below was harrowing.

Methodically, she began to strip the linen off the bed. Two sheets and two blankets gave her an adequate rope, and she tied them together carefully. It had begun to rain when she cautiously lowered her makeshift rope out the window. Praying that all her knots would hold, she swung out the window and braced her feet against the stone of the house. Slowly, foot by foot, she lowered herself toward the vicious rocks below. In minutes she was on the ground.

Her boots slipping on the wet rocks, she carefully made her way along the water. There was a shout from the house, then more voices, and she realized they had found her escape route. The rain poured down as she struggled up the shore to the narrow road that led off the point to Coldingham. Pulled off the road was a wagon with a broken wheel. Its back was piled with empty sacks. Catherine heard the noise of pursuit behind her and made a run for the cart. Without a second thought, she flattened herself on the floor and pulled the sacks over her. She lay, tense from the confinement, but sustained by the fire of her fury. In a matter of seconds she heard Ian's voice. "Yes, she can swim. But the sea is brutal today. She must have either gone along the coast or up this road." There was the sound of horses' hooves, then Ian's voice again. "I'll take the coast. Jock, you take the road. If you find her, bring her back."

"Aye, my lord." The sound of horses moving off, then silence. Catherine waited for a few moments, then peeked out from underneath her sacks. They smelled regrettably of fish.

There was no one in sight and thankfully she climbed out of the wagon. The rain poured down. Her hair streamed down her neck, her boots squelched, and her clothes clung to her, but she plodded on, hoping to make it to Coldingham before she was caught again.

It was this drenched and determined figure who confronted Allandale as he rode toward St. Abb's. For a moment he couldn't believe his eyes. Then he was off his horse and running toward her. "Catherine!"

She thought for a moment he was an hallucination. It wasn't possible he could be here. But then he was before her, his black hair streaming with rain, his eyes bright in a surprisingly tan face. She lifted her arms to him. "James. Oh James." Then his mouth covered hers and blotted out the rest of the world. There was rain on his lips and the cool wetness of rain in his hair under her hands. His lips and body clung to him, and she felt her heart begin to race wildly. After a long moment he resolutely put her away from him. His voice shook, "This is a very dangerous activity for the open road, my love."

She swayed for a moment, then regained her balance. "I imagine so," she said uncertainly. Then, more strongly, "However did you get here, James?"

"That is a long story, and you're freezing. Let's get out of this bloody rain first." As he spoke he guided her steps toward his horse, then boosted her into the saddle. In a minute he was up behind her, and the horse was turned around to head back toward Coldingham.

"One of Ian's men is looking for me along this road," she informed him.

"I hope he finds us. I'd like to meet him." He felt her shiver and drew her closer into his arms. With a startled note in his voice, he said, "What on earth is that smell?"

Catherine's laugh pealed out. "Fish, James. I hid in a wagon and covered myself with some old sacks. I'm afraid they had last been used as a wrapping for fish."

He laughed, too, but his voice sounded odd. "You stayed hidden in a wagon, Catherine?"

"Yes, I did." Then, her tone triumphant, she repeated. "Yes, I did! I was so angry, James, that I couldn't think of anything except escaping. I wanted to *kill* Ian! When I woke up in that room, and he told me what he was planning to do, I just saw red. Even when he kissed me, I . . ."

"He kissed you? Is that *all* he tried to do?"

Catherine turned to look into his face. What she saw there frightened her, and she hastened to add, "That's all he did, James. I gave him a vicious kick in the shins, and he went away."

His laugh sounded oddly breathless. "You seem to have managed quite well, my love."

She nodded vigorously, then sneezed. "Oh God. This rain! Where are we going, James?"

"I saw an inn in Coldingham when I passed through. We'll stop there."

She nodded and pressed closer to him. "Good. I'm freezing to death."

It didn't take Allandale long to arrange for a room. He brought Catherine upstairs and asked her what she wanted. "Some hot water," she told him.

"I'll have them send the maid up. I'm going to see about the horse and find out if cousin Ian's henchman has been here yet."

In ten minutes there was a tub of hot water standing before the fire in Catherine's room. Gratefully, she shed her soaked clothes and submerged herself. The heat of the water soaked into her bones and, remembering Allandale's comment about the fish, she washed her hair. She found an extra shirt of Allandale's in his saddlebag and put it on. The maid took her clothes away to dry them.

She was drying her hair in front of the fire when he returned. He looked at her, her long legs bare beneath his shirt, the fire outlining her body through the thin fabric, and felt his breathing alter. She continued to towel her still-wet hair. "Did you find out anything about Ian's man?"

"No."

"Just as well," she said, and reached for his brush. She began to run it through her shining, damp hair. "You never told me how on earth you found me, James."

"No." His voice was harsh. "I think I'd better get out of here, Catherine. I'll see if they have a room for me."

She put down her brush and looked at him. He had taken off his wet coat, but rain drops still clung absurdly to his lashes. "There is plenty of room here," she said.

He made a small movement with his hands, then was still again. "I won't be able to stop this time, Catherine."

With that she came to him. "I don't want you to," and slid her arms about his neck. In one swift motion he picked her up and brought her to lie on the bed.

What blazed up then between them was as fierce and bright and elemental as lightning. They came together with the pure passion of utter need, all thought suspended save the necessity of their love. All of the frustration and pain of the last year was washed away in this clear fire. Afterward, they lay for a moment, looking at each other. Then Catherine's joyous laugh pealed out and in a moment Allandale's followed.

"My love," he said when he had got his breath again, "you are a miracle."

"Thank you," she said, the bubble of joy still lighting her face. She held out her arms and he gratefully pillowed his head on her shoulder. He had been in the saddle for over twenty-four hours. In two minutes he was asleep.

Catherine looked down at the black head lying so still on her shoulder. She rested her lips on his thick, silky hair and for a moment felt toward him as she felt toward Eileen. "My love," she whispered, "oh, my love." Then she too fell asleep.

When she awoke he was lying propped on one elbow, watching her. The look on his face sent a shiver all through her. "Do you know," he said to her, his voice deeper than usual, "can you possibly know what you mean to me?"

"Yes," she answered gravely. "Because I know what you mean to me."

With that he bent and kissed her eyes and then her mouth. Very slowly this time he started making love to her. In ecstasy and delight she turned to him, giving without reserve the joy of her body. Before it had been as if a raging flood had carried them away. This time she felt the individual waves, shimmering through her like the pure high notes of a piano, until the piercing white sweetness was almost more than she could bear. Then he was with her, and the waves were crashing and crashing, leaving her clinging to him, breathless and shaken.

Allandale held her closely, her long hair falling across his chest and covering them both. The depth and strength of Catherine's response had moved him profoundly. He had never truly understood the meaning of the words "giving oneself" until now. The joy she found with him she gave, with total generosity and honesty, in wonder and delight, back to him.

It was a night of miracles for both of them. The last barrier had been broken. What had been wrought by violence had been broken by violence, also. "Poor Ian," Catherine said at one point. They were lying propped up on pillows, holding hands and talking.

Allandale held her hand to his face for a moment. "Poor Ian," he agreed. "I never thought I'd say that, but I feel sorry for the poor devil."

Catherine shook her head. "I still can't believe what he did. Grandpapa's death must have shaken him even more than I thought."

Allandale's long mouth curved and he looked at her, gray eyes glinting. "I understand very well why he tried to kidnap you. I can't say I blame him."

"James!" She sat up and stared at him in indignation. But he just laughed and reached out to pull her down again. Safe in the circle of his arm, she rested her cheek on his shoulder. Gently, his hand caressed her hair.

"My heart, I imagine Ian feels about you pretty much the way I do. I just happened to be lucky enough to get you."

"Ian is just a boy," came Catherine's muffled voice. "He'll find someone else."

Allandale doubted it. But it was not a topic he had any intention of pursuing. His hand moved from Catherine's hair down the length of her body. She shivered in anticipation. After all, there were far more interesting things to do than talk about Ian Maxwell.

XXII

My soul hath her content so absolute
That not another comfort like to this
Succeeds in unknown fate.

—WILLIAM SHAKESPEARE

When next she woke it was morning, the bright sun streaming in the window of their room. Catherine sat up and stretched luxuriously, then she turned to Allandale. His black hair was rumpled and hung over his forehead. His lashes, ridiculously long for a man's, lay on tan cheeks. Catherine felt tears of tenderness sting her eyes, then bent and kissed him. He awoke instantly, his eyes totally alert. She grinned at him. "I'm not the enemy, James. Good morning. I'm starving."

He looked aggrieved. "How can you talk of food at a time like this?"

Catherine's stomach growled, and she patted it reassuringly. "Poor thing, you'll be fed soon, I promise." She looked at him sternly. "I can talk of food, James, because I haven't had any in twenty-four hours."

He looked struck. "Now you mention it, I haven't eaten in longer than that."

Catherine ruthlessly pulled the sheet back. "To the dining room!" But, having jumped out of bed, she looked around in perturbation. "Where are my clothes?"

"Good point, my love. When last I saw you dressed you were wearing my shirt. What happened to your clothes?"

"I gave them to the maid to dry." She hopped back into bed and pulled the covers up to her chin. "James, can you find the maid and see what happened to them?"

His mouth twitching with suppressed laughter, he agreed, and pulling on his own clothes, rang the bell. When the maid appeared she brought a pile of clothes with her, as well as a pot of tea. With deep relief Catherine recognized her garments. Allandale was interested in them as well. "I must admit, my love, I failed to notice your attire yesterday." He looked appreciatively at the tall, slim figure of his wife, clad in breeches, boots, and shirt.

"I was riding, *ventre à terre*, to what I supposed to be your deathbed," she told him tartly. "I think I am dressed most appropriately."

"Do you ride astride?" he asked seriously.

"Yes."

"Why did you never ride that way at Barton Abbey?"

She flushed. "I didn't think it would be proper."

He raised an eyebrow. "Don't be an ass."

With that she laughed and, linking an arm in his, headed him toward the door. "I'll be an ass dead of starvation if I don't get some food soon."

"I get the distinct feeling," he said as she propelled him down the stairs, "that I'd better feed you."

"What I love about you, James," she said amicably, "is the way you take a hint." They entered the coffee room, flushed with love and laughter.

After an enormous breakfast, Catherine put down her fork and heaved a sigh. "I couldn't eat another morsel to save my life," she declared.

Allandale looked at the chiseled perfection of his wife and shook his head in amazement. "For someone who looks as if she lived on champagne and peaches, you put away a healthy meal, my love."

"I know," she said complacently. "I always had a good appetite." Daintily she wiped her fingers on her napkin, then looked at him again. "Poor Papa must be frantic, James. We'd better get back to Newlands as soon as possible."

He frowned. "I know. I'm going to arrange to hire a

carriage; it will be far more comfortable and won't take that much more time. But first, Catherine, what is to be done about Ian?"

Color flared in her cheeks. "What do you mean?"

"Do we just leave him in the lurch, as it were?"

"Do you want to invite him to accompany us?" she asked indignantly.

"No," he answered slowly. "But I think I ought to see him before we leave."

"I don't know. He may inadvertently have done us a good turn by his crazy behavior, but I confess I still see red every time I think of it. Ian, my cousin Ian, tried to kidnap me!" She looked so much like a ruffled kitten that he had to laugh.

"I know, my heart," he said soothingly. "But I think I'd better see him anyway."

She looked uneasy. "You won't do anything foolish, James?"

He rose from the table. "No, Catherine, I won't do anything foolish. Why don't you go pack my poor meager gear back into the saddlebag, and as soon as I return, we'll be off." He watched her slowly leave the room, then went out to the stable himself. He arranged to hire a carriage, then headed back to St. Abb's.

The day was as bright and clear as yesterday had been dark and stormy. The North Sea was calm, reflecting back the light of the day. Seated on the rocky beach, the summer sun striking gold from his blond hair, was Ian Maxwell, now Earl of Carberry.

He didn't hear Allandale until he was almost next to him, then he swung around, startled out of his trance. When he saw who it was, the bright color flamed up in his fair face. "You!" he said chokingly, "how did you get here?"

Allandale propped his foot on a rock and stood regarding Ian measuringly. "I came after Catherine, of course. Did you think I wouldn't?"

"What do you care about Cathy?" Ian flung at him, and resolutely fixed his eyes on the water.

Allandale was silent for a minute, but his gray gaze

never left Ian's face. Finally he said, calmly, "I care a
great deal for Catherine." He paused, then went on,
"Would it be possible, Ian, for any man to live with
Catherine and not come to love her?" Startled, Ian's
blue eyes left the sea and turned to the face of the man
so near him, the man who was Catherine's husband,
the man he hated. The gray eyes held an expression
Ian had never seen in them before. "Well," he said relentlessly, "would it be possible?"

"For most men, no," Ian said grudgingly. Then,
"Where is she?"

"At the inn in Coldingham. She is waiting for me to
return to set out for Newlands. My father-in-law was
dreadfully worried when I left him, and she is anxious
to get back as soon as possible."

Ian spoke with difficulty. "Did she send you to see
me?"

"No." With a swift movement of characteristic
grace, Allandale seated himself on a boulder opposite
to Ian. "Catherine is still rather angry with you, I am
afraid. It is I who wanted to come. You see, Ian," he
spoke slowly, "I rather feel for you in all this." He
smiled at the astonished look on the young face opposite him. "You know," he said carefully, "Catherine
really doesn't understand the kind of emotion she can
provoke in a man."

Ian buried his head in his hands. His voice was
muffled. "She thinks I'm a boy, that I only love her because I haven't met many other girls." He looked up at
Allandale, pain in his eyes. "But that's not true."

"No," Allandale agreed, "I don't imagine it is. But it
would be a kindness to let her think it was."

"I don't understand you."

"I mean, Ian, that I love Catherine and, by some
generosity of fate, she loves me. I realize you may find
that hard to believe. I understand you unearthed the
sad facts that led to our marriage. Nevertheless, it is
true." Allandale's gray eyes held Ian's mercilessly. "We
had a number of difficulties to overcome and, partly
thanks to you, we have done so." He spoke slowly,

with relentless logic. "If you do not wish to alienate Catherine altogether, you must accept this. And if you do not wish to make her deeply unhappy, you must not convey to her the feeling that, because of her, your life has been permanently blighted." Ian's hands gripped together until the knuckles turned white, but his eyes never left Allandale's. "Do you understand what I am saying, Ian?"

Ian's young face looked haggard in the bright light, but his lips were firm and his voice steady. "Yes," he said, "I understand you."

"Good." Allandale rose to his feet. "Go to France, Ian. You need to get away. We shall be at Aix-la-Chapelle in September, then back in London. Come to see us. Catherine may not love you as you want her to, but that doesn't mean she doesn't love you at all. You must be satisfied with that."

Ian looked at him straightly. "Would you be?"

Allandale was honest. "No."

Ian held his eyes, then his blue gaze turned to the sea. His voice was desolate. "I'll go to France."

Allandale looked at the boy seated before him. But there was nothing more he could do. He held out his hand, and Ian rose and took it. Then he turned and made his way back to the road, leaving Ian standing alone on the empty shore.

Catherine was in the courtyard when he returned to the inn. He saw again in his mind's eye that lonely figure on the beach and, before the interested view of two ostlers and the landlord, he kissed her hard. Catherine's cheeks were pink, but she laughed when he released her. "What was that all about?" she asked. But he wouldn't answer.

They arrived at Newlands early the next morning. Sir Francis heard them drive in and ran down the front stairs to greet them. "Cathy, James, thank God!" His eyes went to his son-in-law's face and what he saw there caused him to catch his breath. He turned to his daughter as she reached out to hug him.

"James came to the rescue in the nick of time, Papa." He looked at the beautiful laughing face so close to his and, irresistibly, smiled back. There was a look about Catherine that he had never seen before. Her beauty, always astonishing, was now luminous with an inner radiance. Sir Francis saw her look at Allandale, and thought he understood. His heart rejoiced, but his voice remained carefully stern.

"You had me worried to death. First I get this letter from you intimating that James was at death's door, then James himself turns up for dinner."

"I know," she said sympathetically. "We got back as soon as we could, poor darling. How is my baby?" she continued eagerly.

"Actually, Cathy, she's been rather fussy. I think she misses you."

Catherine looked delighted. "Of course she did, poor love. Come along, James. You haven't seen your daughter in an age."

Allandale smiled at Sir Francis and let himself be steered into the house. Sir Francis heard him say, "Does she still look like me?" as they disappeared up the stairs.

After dinner that evening, Catherine went to the piano. As she ran through some scales, Sir Francis asked Allandale, "How did things go in Spain?"

Allandale's face darkened. "Not too well. There is going to be bloodshed before long."

"What about Aix-la-Chapelle?"

"About the only course of action I can see, sir, is to try to keep the major powers from becoming too tightly allied and ganging up on the smaller nations."

Sir Francis looked thoughtful. "Will that be England's policy?"

"I don't know. But the government has asked me to represent it, and it will certainly be *my* policy."

Catherine looked up from the piano. "Can I come with you to Aix-la-Chapelle?"

"I certainly hope you do, my love." He smiled at

her, his gray eyes strangely alight. "You have a bit of a talent for sowing dissension yourself, I think."

She ignored that. "What about Eileen?"

"They have babies in France too, you know. I don't see why she can't come."

With a radiant smile, she turned back to the piano. Music came pouring into the room, cascading over them in ringing joy. Sir Francis felt tears sting his eyes as he listened to his daughter's magnificent testament of love. Allandale sat perfectly still, his breath almost suspended. When the music ceased, Sir Francis had gone and he rose and went to his wife.

She looked at him, joy running almost visibly in her veins. "Thank you, my heart," he said softly.

She stood before him, her hands lying lightly on his lapels. "I am sorry about Spain," she said.

He returned her clear gaze. "It is not going to be easy, this task we've set ourselves, Catherine. We may very well see all efforts fail and Europe go up in smoke before our eyes." Her steady regard never wavered. "But with you by my side, I don't think there is anything I couldn't face." His hand carressed her cheek. "I love you," he said, "God, how I love you."

She closed her eyes as his mouth came down on hers. The joy that raced in her veins ignited into flame. When he finally raised his head, her voice sounded breathless. "I never understood what Blake meant before."

"Blake?"

"Yes. 'Tyger! Tyger! Burning bright/ In the forests of the night. . . .' I never knew what he meant until now. He's right. It is burning and beautiful, and fearful, too."

His arm came around her shoulders and he began to walk her toward the door. "I suggest we go upstairs and discuss this further, my love."

A smile turned up the corners of her mouth. "A very sensible suggestion, James. By all means, let us pursue the matter to its conclusion." They went up through the quiet house to their room.

ABOUT THE AUTHOR

JOAN WOLF is a native of New York City who presently resides in Milford, Connecticut, with her husband and two young children. She taught high school English in New York for nine years and took up writing when she retired to rear a family. THE COUNTERFEIT MARRIAGE is her first book.